Rainbows and Sunshine...
and Zombies

P. A. Douglas

This book is dedicated to Frank. Thanks for being my friend.

Author's Note:

Although Southeast Texas is a real place, none of the characters, places, or things in this book is real. This is a work of fiction. Any people, places, or things that may resemble actual life in this story are strictly by coincidence. If you live in the Carcinogenic Coast near where this story takes place, don't bother looking for a familiar bar or safe place away from the inevitable future. Because, in this world, we all die sooner or later.

Author Acknowledgements

To Dane Hatchell, Blake Lowe, Sarah Vonkain, Jim Agpalza, Richard Laymon, Kevin L. Donihe, and Oprah. To everyone at Severed Press. To all of my friends who read my work because they feel obligated. And to you, the reader... thanks for your obligation-free choice to pick up this book. I hope you enjoy this little journey. I know I did. Otherwise, I wouldn't have wasted my time writing it.

Other Severed Press Titles by P. A. Douglas
The Old One
Killer Koala Bears from Another Dimension
The Dark Man
Hitchers
Epidemic of the Undead
Rancid
Watchers

.

CHAPTER ONE

Have you ever found yourself wondering, *'why am I holding this lit stick of dynamite,'* while at the same moment finding yourself watching a co-worker smash a dead man in the face with a freaking dead blow hammer?

Yeah, I can't honestly say I ever expected that one either, but here I am just the same. Dynamite stick, currently ignited, I might add. The fuse is shrinking ever closer to my hand and the base of that life extinguishing stick. Frank the Tank swings repeatedly. The thick biceps and pectoral muscles tighten and bulge with each plunge of vigor. The dead man, and what remained of his face, now just a clump of mush and pus-red gore.

But before I ram this stick of lit dynamite into the dead, faceless man's chest, and Frank the Tank and I escape to the safety of our truck, let's backtrack a little. Bring you up to speed.

First off, Frank the Tank's real name is actually Frank… the… Tank. No, he didn't get the name as some type of a nickname for being so brutal or massive. Most people assume that's a made up name for him because of how he's ripped. That's not the case, but hey, the muscles don't hurt. Could you imagine being blessed with a physique as gloriously toned as his and being named something like Ruben, instead? Walking around flashing your muscles and flexing your pecks to a nickname like Sandwich? That just wouldn't cut it. Worse, what if you had a name like Frank the Tank, but you were in fact built nothing like a tank. Hi there, this is my friend, Frank the Tank. He likes quiet time and reading. In fact, he has never once bludgeoned someone to death just by flexing. Or Gillie the Guillotine—the one man who never decapitated anyone... Ever.

Yeah, that just wouldn't work.

Frank the Tank was named after his father, Gus the Bus. It's just genetics—his real name, a perfect match. A man of muscle and brutal rage.

Once the two of us started working together, I tried coming up with a cool name like his for myself. Honestly, it was a disaster. There's not much out there that really rhymes with Pat, like a tank, or a submarine. Pat the hat, the bat, the cat, the fat, the rat. The list is endless. And sadly, none of them just seemed to stick. Until Frank the Tank gave me a nickname.

My name is Pat, but most everyone these days calls me Tattoo.

If you're wondering what brought on a name like that... well, then just look at the book cover. That should explain it.

Now that you've taken a look at the cover, you're probably wondering why two people like us would even team up. We're so different; it seems as if we would have nothing in common.

In a lot of ways, this is true.

But with the end of the world a lot has changed. And you would be surprised who ended up getting along with who just for the sake of survival.

That's right. The end of the world. I said it. Armageddon. This is a post-apocalyptic world ruled by the dead. Hence, the dead blow hammer, face bludgeoning by Frank the Tank, and the dynamite in my hand. With the end of the world came a new set of rules. A new order to the system that fell with the rise of the 'Dees.'

We call them Dees because they're dead, but you probably already knew that. 'Dead Heads' was already taken by some trippy LSD band from the 60's, and the Flower Power movement. So that was ruled out, and calling them the living dead just became too much work. Too many syllables.

Dees works just fine.

And it caught on, too.

The whole world is calling them that now.

After more than five years of chaos, the world can finally agree on something. I find that crazy. The world falls apart, and then we come together and at least agree on one thing. Dees for zombies. In the end, I think that's how it got out of hand. Everyone was too busy blaming each other instead of doing anything about it. The Russians blamed the Canadians. The Americans blamed some place I can't even pronounce, ruled by people with towels on their heads. Africa and Mexico blamed the US President. It just went in a big fat circle. Finger pointing. That's all it was. And all the while, the dead stalked the Earth. Rose out of their graves. Anyone they bit or scratched died. That dead person obviously got up. And it just kept going. It spread like wildfire. Assuming that wildfire can spread pretty fast. I wouldn't know. I've never actually seen a wildfire.

Eventually, the world did put aside their differences and theories and just started looking to eradicate the problem. It's funny how hard one might find it to kill something that's already dead. Needless to say, this little world problem didn't go away overnight.

The problem did eventually get placed in check. But in the game of chess, getting your opponent up against the wall just means you're probably only one move away from getting your own hand chewed off and swallowed.

Trust me. I've seen it happen.

With all that said the Dees were in fact detained… for a time. Cornered and burned. You see, burning them, or blowing them up, is just about the only way to get rid of them. No shots to the head. And a dead blow hammer to the head—same deal. Just slows them down. You could 'Frank the Tank' them in the face with a dead blow hammer via bulging pectorals for a day and a half and they would still get up sooner or later. They may not have a face to do any biting with. In fact, they could be a neck stump of pulpy goo and still get up sooner or later. More than likely sooner than later.

Thus, the dynamite in my hand—the fuse getting that much closer to *go time*.

Now, I know what you're asking yourself. Why is there need of such violence if the world finally cornered and contained the problem? Well, yes… like I said. For the most part this did happen. And for a while everyone thought it was over.

Until it happened.

Until the first person died. No bites. No scratches. And yet, just like that. Dees all over again.

It didn't matter. Natural causes. Boating accident. Work related injury. Car crash. Man, pile-ups on the interstate are the worst. Let me tell you.

Anyway… it came back.

But this time we were ready, kind of.

A new workforce emerged.

Dee extermination.

The competition was pretty high at first. Everyone and their grandmother wanted a piece of the pie. Hell, who wouldn't? With the President backing all of these small business start-ups to ensure the safety of the nation, it was inevitable. But eventually it died off. People either died trying or realized the risk, and got out while they still had all their limbs.

Smart move if you ask me, considering the fact that I could lose an arm if I don't throw this dynamite sometime soon.

But all that was a few years ago. Things have settled down and the competition has dwindled. Across the United States there are probably thousands of companies like the one we work for. That however, doesn't matter. What matters is that down here in Southeast Texas, there are only three companies competing for number one on Dee patrol.

And at the end of the day, Armageddon or not, you still got bills to pay.

Frank the Tank and I... we work for a company called I-Corpse. And down here, in the carcinogenic coast of Southeast Texas, we *are* the '*A*' team.

CHAPTER TWO

"Frank," I said, eyes wide as I glared at the dynamite in my left hand. "Give it a rest! Go time!"

Frank the Tank swung the dead blow hammer once... two more times—blood jutting from beneath the blunt end of the hammer as it made impact with the Dee's mangled face. His bulging arms were glistening with the crimson gunk that spurted from the Dee's pulpy head.

"I don't much want to have my hand blown up, man. Let's go!"

Frank the Tank smiled, got to his feet, and crossed his arms. He looked like a freak of nature with those massive arms. His muscles made the 30 pound dead blow hammer look smaller than it would have looked if it were in my hands.

"What are you waiting for, Tattoo?" Frank the Tank nodded at the bomb in my hand. "Toss it."

So, I did.

The stick of dynamite left my hand and soared through the air at the mangled Dee on the ground. Just as the explosive landed in the undead corpse's lap, Frank the Tank, and I, dashed across the Wal-Mart parking lot to find safety behind our work truck. I leaned against the front passenger tire breathing heavily. Frank ducked down beside me.

Frank the Tank's phone rang.

Pulling the phone from his shirt pocket, he didn't even seem to notice the blood all over his hands as he pressed the accept call button on the home screen.

"Hey honey… miss you." Frank the Tank paused, his wife obviously on the other end exchanging some form of pleasantries.

While I leaned against the truck, waiting for the bomb to explode, I watched my co-worker on the phone. Watched him hold that little smart phone in his massive hand, his biceps and forearms tearing with bulging veins. You might think the phone would crush under the weight of his bear grip.

It didn't.

I decided to take a peek at the Dee in the Wal-Mart parking lot. I leaned up, looked over the hood of our work truck. The undead corpse started to shuffled. I could see the stick of dynamite getting close to the—

BOOM!

The Dee exploded.

Blood, matted chunks of tattered flesh covered in singed hair, and particles of clothing fabric rained down on the service truck.

Leaning there against the truck, covered in gore, I watched as Frank nodded. "Pick up some milk. I got it." He smiled. "I love you, too."

"Dude," I said, wiping bits of flesh off my shoulders as I stood. "You talk to that woman on the phone any nicer, I think I might vomit."

"Whatever," Frank the Tank said, pocketing the phone. "Let's just clean up this mess. It's almost lunch."

I looked at the clip-watch on my belt. Fifteen to noon. I hadn't realized it was so late in the morning. My stomach grumbled.

As we walked around to the back of the service truck to unroll the water hose and connect it to the pressure valve, I asked, "So, what's for lunch?"

"So..."

"Well?" I replied.

"What is it with you and saying 'so'?" Frank the Tank turned on the pressure valve releasing the water from the reserve on the truck. Water jutted from the hose and did a meek job at spraying down the parking lot gore. "It's always 'so' this and 'well' that."

"So..."

"Well?"

We both laughed.

"I don't know, man," I said. "When I say 'so,' it means I have a question. Like—so, what's for lunch? And well... well, it means I have a statement. Well, that was messy. You see? Statements and questions, Frank. They make up sentences. It's called talking. You do know what communication is, right?"

Frank the Tank grunted, turning off the valve for the service truck water reserve. The water slowed to a trickle from the water hose. After we rolled up the hose and put everything away, we climbed into the truck and drove away, leaving most of the exploded Dee still all over the Wal-Mart parking lot.

Frank the Tank drove while I stared out the window, remembering how the city used to be before everything had changed. Before this job. Don't get me wrong. I enjoy the job, and Frank the Tank is my best friend, but that still doesn't change that it kind of sucks now. Things used to be so much better. Easier. Now, life was just an eventuality. Because... despite the fact that no one talked about it, the truth remained. And it was lingering at the back of everyone's mind. That last thought you have just before falling asleep. One day, I would die from a crazy exploding stick of TNT in my hand or from natural causes. Either way, it was inevitable. I would become a Dee. Everyone would, even Frank the Tank. It was just a matter of when. I guess that lingering thought—that reality—it made things in life feel a little numb. Sitting there, looking out the window, it was like life wasn't what it used to be. Now it was more of a dream. A thick fog of the mind that somehow just couldn't be real. Even still, you knew it was never going to change.

"It's just a matter of time," Frank the Tank said.

Looking up, I almost thought he was thinking the same thing as me, but he wasn't. When I turned my attention to him, he was pointing out the window. "What?"

"Just a matter of time before the Cowboys take it to the Super Bowl." He was pointing at a billboard. Three Dallas Cheerleaders in skimpy clothing were pasted on the board. The words, "Taking back the price," were in bold just below the women's ample cleavage.

"You really think they'll even make the playoffs this year, man?" I nodded. "I don't much care for the quarterback they have this year."

Frank the Tank didn't reply. In fact, he didn't even bother asking me where I wanted to eat. Instead, he just pulled into the parking lot of the same old Mexican restaurant that we ate at almost every single day.

It doesn't matter where we eat. Frank the Tank is always going to order the same thing. The combo platter. Sushi bar: combo platter. Chicken Inn: combo platter. Mexican: combo platter. McDonalds: combo platter. I don't even think fast food places have a combo platter. Yet, he still manages to get it.

I stare at the menu while Frank the Tank places his order, his pectorals bulging as if he were going to tear the menu apart while he skimmed it.

"Combo platter and a Coke."

9

"I'll get what he got."

The waiter walked away with the menus.

"So…" I cleared my throat.

"Well…"

"So, you do realize that you order the exact same thing every single place we go, right?"

"That just means I'm a man that knows what he wants."

"I guess." I shrugged my shoulders.

"Like you have any room to talk. Just about everywhere we eat, you just say…" Frank cleared his throat and straightened his back. With a high-pitched whine in his voice, he mocked, "…I'll get what he got."

"So what?" I said. "I just think ordering food is something not worth the effort. Why bother choosing a meal when any meal will do?"

"That doesn't even make sense," Frank the Tank said. "If any meal will do, then I'm sure we can extend lunch break to go pick up some dog food for you. We can even leave the bag in the truck."

"Yeah, yeah, yeah…." I rolled my eyes.

We sat there in silence for a long while, eating chips and dip, and waiting on the combo platters to arrive. Frank the Tank flexed with each chip he took from the bowl. I sank into my chair, my gut bulging out past my belt line. If there was any one person who made me feel out of shape, it was him. By the time the chips were depleted our food arrived.

"Pat, come in. We got a hot one over in Bridge City." The radio on my right hip crackled. It was Ben, the onsite extermination manager.

"Don't answer that, Tattoo. We're on lunch break."

I started to reach for the radio. "Hey, a job's a job. Just because he's probably known about this call for a few hours and decided to wait till he knew we were eating to call it in is beside the point." I answered the radio. "This is Pat. Come in..."

Static.

"Had a house over on 15th and Maple by the Dixie Plus gas station. Fire crew and paramedics already got sent out. The house was full of people."

"Great," Frank the Tank mumbled.

"I know the location," I replied, watching my partner glare at me. "We're on our way."

I latched the radio back into place and picked up my fork.

"What, not in a hurry?"

"Hell no," I said. "My food just got here."

I took a bite, and we enjoyed the rest of our lunch break in silence.

CHAPTER THREE

By the time we pulled up to the burning building in Bridge City, it was too late. The 15 minute nap we took after lunch didn't help matters much either. What matters, I think, is that we did get there. As my high school history teacher used to always tell me—better late than never.

Chaos is really the best way to describe the scene.

What Frank the Tank and I had honestly expected to be just a quaint little home with a few trapped and burning soon to be Dees was nothing close to small. It was a set of town houses. Three conjoining homes that formed one large three story structure. All of it up in smoke. For the most part, it appeared the fire department had done their job in quenching the flames. The townhomes, however, didn't get saved. Small fires still burned in various windows, but other than that, the charred remains of the building were dilapidated. The first truck and one paramedic ambulance were still present on the scene. The crew for either vehicle, on the other hand, was another story. I didn't see firemen or paramedics anywhere. What I did see were a lot of Dees roaming aimlessly. A lot of them freshly covered in the blood of their victims.

Just from the mere seconds of pulling up on the scene, it was easy to place what exactly went down. One of the townhomes caught on fire engulfing all three into one singular blaze. The homes of at least two of the three had been occupied during the rescue efforts. I came to this conclusion by the numerous Dees I saw shambling about in the yard and street—their flesh burnt to crisps, blackened to stink in the heat.

The other townhome had a larger number of zombies that now milled about the surrounding area, couldn't have been anything other than passersby. People standing by with nothing better to do than watch the buildings go up in flames. Between the dozen charred corpses walking around and the other mangled and bloodied Dees in the area, some of which were walking toward us, I had my number guessed at somewhere around 40 corpses. One or two of them were dressed as firemen. So, that could only mean the firemen were overrun, which led to things getting out of hand.

With the townhouses still sizzling in the background, the fire truck to our left, and the ambulance to our right, Dees took notice.

At least ten of them started shambling toward the truck, their arms raised, necks craned in strange angles, eyes wide and their mouths agape. Blood and drool slid down blood covered jaws and chins.

My radio cracked. "Pat… come in."

Unhooking the radio, I held it to my mouth—my eyes watching the undead amble closer to the service truck. "Go ahead, Ben."

"You guys get that one cleaned up yet? I got another one."

"What is it?"

"The Residential Suites in Nederland. Had another one drop," Ben's voice popped and hissed against the static.

"That place doesn't have a contingency plan for this type of thing yet? Last time we went there, they said they were getting things under control. I'm tired of going to that place, Ben. It smells like rotten eggs in there."

"There's nothing wrong with a little residual income. It helps pay the bills. You still want me signing my name at the bottom of those checks I hand out every week, don't you?"

"The old folks home, again?" Frank the Tank rolled his eyes.

I shrugged at Frank the Tank, and then clicked the button on the radio. "Okay, give us a little bit and we'll be there."

The call ended.

A Dee stepped up to the driver's side door and slammed a bloody hand against the window. I jumped, and Frank the Tank laughed.

"Shut up, man. Not cool," I said, watching the Dee smear crimson across the window. "I'm not cleaning the truck this time. I did it the last three times in a row."

The zombies outside moaned with excitement.

"You want to flip a coin for it?" Frank the Tank reached into his pocket.

The Dee at the door banged against the glass.

"Dude, don't even try. It's your turn, and you know it. Besides, if you think I haven't figured out that your quarter is rigged, then think again."

Frank the Tank laughed, tossing the quarter up, and then catching it. He caught it so tightly that I was surprised it didn't crumble into dust.

"You ready?"

I nodded, reaching for my door handle.

"Since there are so many of them out there, let's do the O.K. Corral."

"Dude, no offence, but the only way I'm running that play is if you actually stick with the script. That time we ran the O.K. Corral you left me standing in the middle of a field surrounded by Dees. Not cool at all."

But he wasn't listening.

Frank the Tank was already kicking his door open. The zombie that had been pressed against the glass fell back on its ass as he stepped out of the truck. By the time my partner's feet landed on the ground he was swinging the dead blow hammer into the face of an approaching ghoul.

I leaned forward and reached over my shoulder, unhooked the shotgun from the rack behind me, and stepped out of the truck.

You could still hear the townhouse fire sputtering in the wind.

CHAPTER FOUR

The shotgun recoiled in my arms. My shoulders kicked, and the report reverberated off the surrounding townhomes.

The zombie I was aiming at fell to the grass in front of the fire truck, its chest bursting with wet reds and pinks as it fell back. With the closest zombie to me down, I turned and ran, made my way to the back of the truck, and quickly climbed into the bed.

I looked out at the yard.

Frank the Tank was on his knees swinging his hammer. Although most of the Dees approaching were still a safe distance back, two zombies staggered a little too close to my partner for comfort.

"Frank, heads up!"

He looked up, quit bludgeoning the zombie before him, and rose to pursue the zombie in front of him. It was one of the charred Dees. It was blackened to a crisp from head to toe. There was no way to determine gender, because it was so mangled. As if not even fazed by the stench of burnt flesh, Frank the Tank stepped forward and slammed the hammer down on the burnt Dee's skull. It caved in, and the ghoul fell to the ground. Dust and an endless cloud of crust fluttered in the air. The burnt flakes glided down, some of the blackened bits clinging to the hammer.

With the shotgun at the ready, I cocked the barrel discharging the spent shell, and then pulled the trigger. The other Dee that closed in on Frank the Tank took the hit in the shoulder. It staggered back a few steps, but that was about it. It froze for a moment to maintain balance and then began its slow pursuit once more toward my partner.

"I got it," Frank the Tank said.

With the empty shell ejected, I chambered two more, and then set the shotgun aside. Dropping to my knees, it was time for the O.K. Corral.

The ropes and hooks were where I had left them. By the looks of it, they missed their last rinse down. The hooks were covered in crusty chunks. They smelled putrid. Whatever. It was going to have to do. I stole a quick glance out at the front yard between the fire truck and the ambulance. Excluding the dead woman with gnashing teeth that Frank the Tank was currently swinging like a baseball bat—her head slamming against the side of the fire truck—I took a quick inventory of how many I could see and their location in the yard. Most of them were closing in on my partner.

After counting what hooks was already tied into place on the roughly 100 foot rope, I tied in a few more. I was in a hurry, so I didn't actually count them. What I had wasn't enough, but it would be a start.

With the end of the long rope in one hand, I stood to my feet in the back of the truck and shouted.

"Soap on a rope!"

Frank the Tank turned toward me still in mid swing, the female Dee's head crashing into the side of the ambulance. His flexing arms dropped her as he turned to me. Tossing one end of the rope, he caught it.

I pulled the rest of the rope off of the truck so as to keep the various hooks attached to it from getting caught on anything. In all, I probably had about fifteen hooks tied in various places on the rope. These hooks were connected to said rope by a smaller, shorter cord, which allowed me to move around doing my thing. You see… Dees are slow. They amble about in not much of a hurry. Yes, in numbers they can corner you and cause a crap ton of problems. But so long as you stay on the move and know how to dodge their out stretched arms and snapping jaws, it's not too hard to deal with them. As much as I want to say I came up with the O.K. Corral, I didn't. Frank the Tank did, and rightfully so, because without him, I personally wouldn't be able to pull this play off. Sure, running around the yard and hooking Dees in the face or under the collarbone until I run out of hooks—all the Dees now locked together by one common thread—I just don't have the muscle to pull it off. That's where Frank the Tank comes in. I-Corpse is the only company in the area that even has a move like this one. Hell, the company we work for is the only one that has a lot of things. They don't call us the A-team for nothing. Even if our competitors decided to give this play a try, I don't see them having the muscle required to pull it off.

Therefore, like every other time before, I run around, hooking one zombie after another with the big meat hooks, doing my best to stay a safe distance away. All the while, Frank the Tank holding one end of the rope. He's got a grin on his face, because he likes this play. If you don't enjoy what you do then why do it… right?

One hook punctures the back of a Dee's head. Blood spurts out spraying across the grass just as the pointed end penetrates the eyes socket and pops out.

I run around doing this until all the hooks are secure.

One zombie gives me the slip twice, and I have to side step-dance around him a few times to get a stick with the hook. It jabs right through the jugular. The zombie's moans become an instant rasp of gargling sounds.

"Man slam!" I shout.

Frank the Tank yanks on the rope.

Did I mention that Frank the Tank loves to fish? Like that's pretty much what he does just about any weekend we have off. Something about revving the engine of his boat. Sinking the line. And waiting through the peace and quiet for that bite. The catch of the day. He says it's tranquil. I think that might be why he likes the O.K. Corral so much.

But trust me. This move is anything but tranquil. It's downright brutal.

Like I said, Frank the Tank tugged on the rope.

All fifteen or so zombies latched in stumbled to the ground around us.

Frank the Tank laughs and yanks again, but this time he's running. He keeps on running until the rope is stretched out straight and all the zombies are in a line. By the time I make it back to the truck, most of the zombies are back on their feet. I can still hear my partner laughing when I dump into the driver's seat and back the truck up to where he's at. In the rearview mirror, Frank the Tank tugs on the rope again—this time with everything he's got. All the zombies tied onto his line lunged intentionally toward him. The face plants and belly flops are atrocious. It makes my stomach churn just watching them collide with the ground that hard. It reminds me of the time I was riding my skateboard down the Rainbow Bridge. Halfway down, one of my front wheels rolled over a rock, and I came to an abrupt and unpleasant stop. I think you get the idea. Only I didn't come down on grass. If these people weren't dead already, I could see them not feeling too hot right about now.

I stopped the truck, and Frank the Tank tied his end of the tope to the back bumper. He walked around to the driver's side, and I rolled down the window.

"I don't think so, dude." I shook my head. "You drove the O.K. Corral the last two times."

"Yeah, so?" Frank the Tank said, walking up to the door. "I'm the driver."

"Not cool, man. Come on."

"Flip for it?"

"I thought we already went over that?"

Frank shrugged. "Can't blame me for trying."

I looked in the side mirror. The zombies were getting to their feet. "They're getting up."

"If you drive, you run the bag."

"Now how the hell is that fair? I run the bag regardless."

Frank the Tank smiled. "Hey, somebody's got to do the paperwork."

"Heck, I could do the paperwork."

Rolling his eyes, my co-worker walked around to the passenger side and got in. I tightly gripped the wheel, and we took off.

If you've never dragged a dead body behind a truck going 50 miles an hour there's really only one word to describe it: messy. What Dees weren't hooked onto the bumper, stepped out into the road chasing after us. This made them an easy target for the front bumper. We went up and down the road slamming into walking corpses left and right. The service truck bounced as each tire rolled over them. In the rearview mirror, I could see a trail of crimson the length of the rope still tied to the bumper.

Once the fun was over, I stepped out of the truck and opened one of the side doors. Removing a sleeve of large black trash bags, I began to run the bag—or clean shit up, if you will.

Frank the Tank sat in the luxury of the service truck's AC and did paperwork. At least that was what he said. Looked more like he was taking a nap to me.

CHAPTER FIVE

"How long have you worked for me, Ben?"

Ben, the onsite crew manager for I-Corpse, cleared his throat. "Well, I… um…"

"You know, Ben. Things are going well for the company, don't you think?"

Ben just sat in his chair, stiff and silent.

Steve Tingbum took a seat across from Ben and lit up a cigarette. Leaning back in his chair, he smiled. Smoke from the cigarette in his left hand fluttered up and into his face, but he didn't seem to mind. Didn't even flinch or bat an eye.

The room was still.

The main office of the company was located in downtown. The center of it all. Steven Tingbum was like that. Location. Location. Location. The man knew how to run a business. He was smart, and he knew it. He was also generous, which would give Ben no real reason to be scared or nervous during the current little impromptu meeting they were having. Even still, he was, and Steve knew it too. Ben knew that he knew it. Steve could read people. Knew when they were lying, telling the truth, or just downright uncomfortable.

Ben fidgeted in his office chair.

Steve smoked and smiled.

Ben's office space was outside next to the service trucks that the onsite crew took out. The building was a small mobile trailer much like a mobile home or classroom, only smaller. It was just big enough for his desk, a computer, the phone, and a bathroom. His desk was cluttered with papers from unfiled jobs that Frank the Tank and I did during the week. Yes, to answer the question, I am still narrating the story, but how could I be telling this part of the story if I wasn't even there? Don't worry about it. Ben and Steve are having a little pow-wow that I know nothing about, and I am still telling the story. It's called the magic of narration in storytelling, so get over it.

Anyway, the paperwork is a mess on his desk. The four walls are bare except for one lone calendar beside the desk that hasn't been flipped to the right month in almost 16 weeks. And that's pretty much Ben's job. He sits in his office and takes calls. He doesn't hunt down jobs or anything like that. Just sits there and waits for the phone to ring. When it rings, he gets the info and quotes the job. Then, he calls the A-team—that's us—and we take care of it.

But that's irrelevant.

Back to the impromptu meeting that I don't actually know about.

"Well, have they or have they not?"

"What?" Ben asked, keeping his hands busy with the pen in his lap.

"The company, Ben. Haven't you heard a word I've said? How do you feel things have been going with the company?"

"Good, Sir. Real good. Pat and Frank do a great job. The best in the business, hands down. We're lucky to have them."

"That's just it, Ben. Things are going too well."

"Wha... what do you mean?" Ben leaned forward in his chair, no longer interested in the pen he was holding.

Steve puffed on his cigarette a few times and exhaled. His expression was that of ecstasy. "You see..." Steve started, "I own and operate my coming and goings with precision."

"Yes, you do."

"Let me finish, Ben. It's rude to interrupt." Steve stubbed what was left of his cigarette into an ashtray on the desk and leaned back. "As I was saying, precision, Ben. All the companies I own help feed one another. The chain of restaurants helps feed the city. The greenhouse fields help feed the restaurants. The dimwits you have working for you help keep the people feeling safe so that they're willing to go to the restaurants. But more important than feeling safe is being afraid."

"I don't follow, Sir."

"Doesn't surprise me at all, Ben. Your little brain trying to wrap itself around something as complex as economics. Don't strain yourself on my account."

"But what does fear have to do with anything? We keep the streets from getting overrun. That's what we're paid to do."

"Yes... in a way."

"I'm still lost."

"Let me place it in terms you might be able to grasp." Steve tapped his fingers on the arm of his chair. "We want to keep people afraid. Your little A-team, or whatever you call it, is doing their job too well. If people begin to think the streets are truly safe again, then they might start thinking it's safe to live outside the borders of our city. Feeling safe means people leaving to reconnect with loved ones, or better yet, becoming freethinkers themselves. People like that go to work for themselves. If the people of this city keep thinking they need to keep working for me to stay safe, then so be it. A city completely rid of Dees is only going to provoke the citizens to get comfortable and start thinking for themselves again."

"So, what am I supposed to do?"

"It was fine when we started. Matt and Larry were good for us then. They helped get things under control."

"You mean Pat and Frank?"

"Whatever, Ben. The muscle guy and the one with all the tattoos. That's beside the point. What I'm getting at here is more important. Pat and Frank were good for the city… for a time. Now they're hindering my goals. They were good for the area when we were constantly overrun. But now… with things finally at a manageable level, it's time to think outside the box. Less clean up and more fear."

"Manageable? We get called out nonstop almost every day of the week, Sir."

"Almost," Steve lingered on the word. "Almost every day. Nowadays, the only Dees we come across are accidental death or health issues. The days of protecting our borders and wondering when the next rot wave was coming are over. And people are starting to think the world outside this town is safe again. We can't have that. We need to strike fear in the streets again. Keep the citizens loyal. Prevent them from leaving. Keep them shopping at my stores, buying at my greenhouses, and eating at my restaurants. And that's not going to happen if your two goons keep doing such a stand up job. A clean street to these people means a clean slate, and that means new competition. New businesses coming in thinking they can compete with my prices, and they will. That is… if your two dimwits keep things up."

"What do you want me to do about it? Get them to back off on calls? I can stop answering the phone every time if rings. Is that it?"

"No, the time for those types of measures has passed. What we need is drastic."

"Then, what should I do? Tell them to take a few weeks off?"

"I want you to do nothing, Ben." Steve stood from his chair and ran his hand down the creases of his shirt to straighten out the wrinkles. "It's already been taken care of. I've got my men on it as we speak."

CHAPTER SIX

The nursing home ended up not being that big of deal, which was honestly a surprise considering. Just about every time we've been out to the place it's been a disaster. Just think about it. Old man falls and breaks a hip. Or at least that's what they think. Orderly leans in to help assist. Boom! Bitten, right then and there. It's a done deal after that. The old man and the orderly turned Dees roam the halls of the home, bumping into other old people and orderlies. You see, the thing about zombies is that they're slow. You would think that's a good thing, but in the end old people are just as slow if not slower. How sad is that? Get run down by a shambling ghoul while I make my escape one hobbling step forward at a time on my trusty cane. Tennis balls may or may not be included.

But this time is wasn't like that. We didn't walk up to the front door and find the place ransacked with the dead. A cute little red head orderly met us at the door, in fact. Tight little white orderly suit matching all the curves of her supple figure. Kind of made me look forward to getting old.

"You here to take care of Mr. Bennett?" She moved a strand of red hair out of her flushed face.

It was as if she had run down a flight of stairs to greet us.

"Yes..." Frank the Tank said, beating me to the door. "Can you tell us what happened?"

"Mr. Bennett had a heart attack, I think," she said. "Tomorrow was going to be his eighty-seventh birthday."

"Has he gotten to anyone else?" I asked.

"He did." She nodded, her eyes frantic. "A co-worker named Carl. He was making his rounds, replacing bedpans in the rooms."

"And..."

Frank the Tank looked back at me. We were waiting for the kicker. The point in the story where this lovely little nurse in all her spender would tell us she was the only one to make it out alive. It wouldn't have been a surprise either.

"No..." she breathed. "That was it, I think."

"You think?" Frank the Tank crossed his arms.

"Yeah," she said. "I was walking by and saw the old man—Mr. Bennett—attack Carl. He sat up in his bed and sank his teeth into Carl's throat. There was blood everywhere. It was just awful."

"It always is, miss." I stepped past Frank the Tank to console her. "It'll be okay. It's all over now."

She quivered and shook in my arms, burying her face into my chest. I stole a glance back to Frank the Tank, grinning ear to ear.

The hardest part about the day was when he shut me down after I attempted to get her digits. Oh well. Life goes on. And then you turn into a Dee.

"Then the situation is contained?" Frank the Tank asked.

"Yes," the female orderly said, lifting her eyes to look up at me. "I saw what was happening and did the only thing I could think to do. I locked them both in Mr. Bennett's room. They're still there now."

"You did the right thing," I said, stroking her hair.

She pulled away.

Frank the Tank stepped up, and said, "Lead the way."

"Wait, shouldn't we, like, formulate a plan or something?"

Frank the Tank nodded at me. "Got any suggestions?"

"Two people in a locked room." I stroked my beard. "Hmmm… How about the Duck and Shove?"

"That only works from higher up," Frank the Tank said.

"Oh, it's on the top floor," the pretty orderly said.

All three of us looked up at the fourth floor.

"Looks legit."

Frank the Tank nodded.

The orderly led the way.

Once we got to the top floor and were directed to the room in question, things went pretty smooth. As you probably guessed it, the Duck and Shove is pretty much self-explanatory. I duck. You shove. Although I claim the creative right to this move, I can't proudly say why I came up with it. Clearly, I'm not the same size and stature of my co-worker, and the same can be said about myself back in the day. The days of school and childhood drama. I wasn't really ever the cool kid in school, got picked on a lot by guys like Frank the Tank. The strong prey on the weak. That sort of thing.

You know the drill. Pretty girl comes up and talks to you. You get excited and started talking back. Don't notice the crowd of people gathering around. And you definitely don't notice the guy that sank down behind you on his hands and knees. Totally innocent. And them, *slam*! You get shoved. You fall back, and the entire school laughs in your face. Yeah, but who's laughing now? It's true. I'll admit it. After the fall and the Dees took over—I looked up some names. Old friends and enemies from school, but mostly enemies. Just about all of them dead. Well, not dead, dead. More like dead and back to life Dee style. It made me feel good knowing that I managed to make it, but most of them didn't. Even had the privilege of pulling the In and Up play on one bully. We got called out to an infestation, and sure enough, the Dee they called about was this brute of a jerk from high school that gave me shit almost every day. I told Frank the Tank I wanted to do the In and Up on this guy to get back at him for all the hell he caused me. It was bliss. I stepped in and got the dead dude's attention, and then Frank the Tank came up with a massive uppercut to the jaw with his dead blow. Ripped his head clean off his shoulders.

Anyway, we're not talking about the In and up here, are we? We're talking about the Duck and Shove.

With the door on the fourth floor in front of us, we could hear the grunting moans of two very dead Dees inside the room. Frank the Tank held his arm up to quiet the red headed orderly. The hallway we stood in fell silent.

Frank the Tank listened for a while with his ear to the door. Just when he was sure he knew the threat inside the room was away from the door and not on alert, he gave me the nod. I nodded back.

Frank the Tank kicked the door down with one furious thrust.

Assessing the threat location in the room, I stepped in and leaped across the bed. In no time, I was kneeling down in front of the window.

Frank the Tank charged in football tackle style. Head down. Shoulders out. He crashed into the orderly, who had a blood covered throat and mangled face. Carl crashed backward into me. I braced and felt him topple over. Carl, the dead orderly, kept on falling and he collided with the window. Glass shattered and rained down on my back. Just as soon as I felt the weight of Carl against me, it was gone.

"Coming at you!" Frank the Tank shouted.

I looked up to see him shoving the old man who started the mess in the first place. I braced for impact, felt the boney old man land against me, and then nothing.

When I looked up, Frank the Tank had his hand out to help me to my feet.

"What kind of a plan was that?" the red head orderly asked.

"What matters," I said, "is that it was effective. The two Dees may not be immobilized, but they are definitely immobile. Nothing like a four story drop to break a few bones and keep you from doing much walking around."

"We'll dispose of the bodies after we take a break."

And that's what we did.

The two Dees we shoved out the window lay on the ground outside trying to get up, but they couldn't. Their bones were damaged, and they wouldn't be getting up any time soon, no matter how badly they wanted it.

Frank the Tank and I sat in the AC of the service truck and kicked back with a little peace and quiet.

At some point, I fell asleep.

CHAPTER SEVEN

Frank the Tank's phone rang. He answered it and started talking before it even finished the first set of chimes. His voice jarred me from my sleep.

"Okay, honey, I miss you, too." He paused. "I'll be home soon. Yeah, I'm with Tattoo. We're finishing up the call out at the nursing home. I'll call you when we get back to the shop. Yes..."

Frank the Tank kept with the smoochy-smooch talk on the phone, but I wasn't listening. Straightening myself in the chair, I looked out at the retirement home building. From my vantage point, I could see the two zombies in the grass at the base of the building. They lay there still squirming about, but not actually getting anywhere—their bones for the most part crushed from the fall. The window four stories up appeared to have already been taped over with garbage bags or something like that.

I stared at the two zombies writhing in the grass, and I began to wonder.

Frank the Tank ended his call with his wife. "Kiss, kiss. Call you later."

"So..."

"Well," Frank mocked.

"I was thinking."

"Oh, here we go again, always thinking."

"No, for real," I said, craning my neck to look at him. "What do you think caused all this? The zombies, I mean?"

"Who knows, Tattoo? It's been so long now it could have been anything."

"Well, take a guess. If you had to pick one thing, what do you think is causing it?"

Frank the Tank sat there for a moment in thought. He seemed to stare out the window for a long while looking up at the sky. "The streaks."

"The what?"

"You know," he said, pointing his finger out at the sky with his massive flexing arm, "the streaks in the sky. Before all of this, I don't much remember seeing that stuff, do you?"

"Come to think of it, no I don't." I leaned forward in my seat to get a closer look at the baby blue expanse. "You mean the jet streams? I'm pretty sure that stuff is just residual from flying planes, like the smoke exhaust or something. Like from the tailpipe of your car, but only on a plane."

"I'm not saying that ain't what it is," Frank the Tank said, "but it seems to be a lot more lately. I read an article that said they were actually spraying stuff in the sky on the weekends. It's for global warming or something like that. They crop dust this stuff worldwide to help cool the earth. You ask me what I think is keeping the Dees in the game? It's that crop dusting junk. That's what..."

"Yeah," I said. "I never thought about that before. Sounds legit."

"Yep. If you keep an eye on it, they seem to spray a lot of that stuff on weekends. I think it's something in those trails." He pointed to the sky again. "Something in those chemicals getting into our systems. Making us wake up after we die."

We both sat there in silence for a while thinking about it.

"I'm surprised Ben hasn't called in another job yet. He's usually on it after lunch."

"Ehh…" I waved a dismissive hand. "We deserve the break."

"What about you… what do you think caused all this?"

"Oh, I don't know, dude. I was just wondering if you had any theories."

Frank the Tank reached into his front pocket and pulled out a can of chewing tobacco.

While I watched him scoop out half the can in one big chunk and stuff it into his mouth, I asked, "Hey, here's one. If you could be anything in the world other than an extermination expert, what would it be?"

Without the slightest bit of hesitation, Frank the Tank said, "Astronaut."

"Really?"

"Yep… did you know that for only three million bucks you can get in a NASA rocket and visit the space station in orbit for three days?"

"Wow, a million bucks a day?"

"Totally worth it if you ask me. I'm saving up for it right now."

"Nice."

"Being up there and seeing how small we really are in the bigger picture would be a mind altering experience."

"For real. That would be awesome."

"Well, since you're big into outer space and what not, what's your take on aliens?"

We sat in the car for a while longer soaking up the AC. We talked about all kinds of stuff like we normally do. Today's topics jumped around a little bit, but not much. We discussed aliens, time travel, the Bermuda triangle, Area 51, Stonehenge, the creation of ultra-sonic wave frequencies and the applications they potentially possessed. Really, it goes on and on.

Eventually, the phone rang again—my co-worker's, not mine. While he played smoochy-kissy face on the phone, I climbed out of the truck. It was time to round up the bodies and dispose of them.

Still feeling a little bummed about not getting the little red headed orderly's number, I opened the side compartment on the truck. Retrieving the hatchet and a few large black bags, it was time to finish the job. I looked back into the cab of the truck to see if he would give me a hand, but Frank the Tank was already off the phone with his wife and doing paperwork for the job.

Shrugging it off, I set to chopping limbs and bagging parts.

Once the bloody mess was done, my clothes covered in gore, the bags made their way into the bed of the truck along with all the bagged bodies from the earlier jobs of the day. It had been a busy day. Generally, most days were. By quitting time, the truck bed would be full to the rim with black garbage bags of bodies. Heads and legs. Torsos and feet. Hands and chins. And yes, seeing as to how destroying the brain doesn't actually kill them, cutting them up doesn't either. Cutting them up just keeps them from becoming a problem. The only sure fire way to get rid of them is to burn the bodies.

And that's what we do with them at the end of the day. Take them back to the shop. Other shop workers run them through the burners.

That's right. We have an entire shop at the shop. A crew of workers is there to make things easier Frank the Tank and me. They do weapon and truck maintenance.

They build new dynamite, which is a good thing, considering I generally go through a few sticks of that stuff a day. They pretty much just keep the wheels greased and the machine that is I-Corpse moving nice and smooth.

Once the bags were tossed in the back with all the rest, I climbed into the passenger seat of the service truck.

I shook my finger wildly to signal I was ready to roll out.

Frank the Tank nodded and jammed the truck into drive.

Since we hadn't heard from Ben yet, the only logical thing to do was drive back to the shop.

We continued our conversation about aliens and how there was aluminum in deodorant strictly for population control. The list goes on and on. The conspiracies, thick.

We were so engrossed in the various topics of our conversation, in fact, that neither of us realized we were being followed.

CHAPTER EIGHT

"What do you mean, *'you've got your men on it?'*" Ben asked, seeing Steve to the door. "What are you planning to do? We can't afford to lose those two. And what you're talking about... well, at least what I think you're talking about—it's murder."

"Now, now." Steve turned toward Ben just as he stepped through the doorway leading out of Ben's office. "How is it murder, if all that my men are doing is merely detaining a couple of Dees? Sad really, losing our top boys at I-Corpse to the job. Sure, employee insurance will go up once I report the incident, but such is business. We can rebuild. We always have."

"But, boss." Ben pleaded, but Steve wasn't hearing it.

Steve finished walking through the door and continued without looking back.

The last thing Ben heard from his employer before he rounded the corner and disappeared from sight was one single word.

Steve's favorite word.

"Toodeloo!"

CHAPTER NINE

"Pat… Frank… come in." It was Ben on the radio.

"About time." Frank the Tank nodded.

Unclipping the radio from my hip, I said, "Hey, boss. Finally got another run? Please tell me it was a drowning at the waterpark or something. I could use a little pick me up after I got shut down by the nurse at the old folk's home."

Frank the Tank smiled, clearly in agreement.

The radio sputtered with static for a moment, and then Ben's panicked voiced said, "No, listen to me. And listen good. Steve… our boss. He's so freaking good at business that he's crunched his numbers and sees a hole in the way he runs things."

"So what? That man is legit," I said. "He can fix it."

"That's just it," Ben replied. "He is fixing it."

"Then what's the problem?" Frank the Tank asked. "Tell him, Tattoo… then what's the problem? Steve's got it under control."

So, I did. "What's the problem? Steve's good at fixing holes in stuff like that. You remember the time he managed to get us like three extra bucks a week on our 401K just because of some dumb rules the President put into place? He's a hole fixer. Let him do his thing."

"That's just it," Ben's voice crackled over the radio. "You're the hole."

Me and Frank the Tank shared a glance, my eyebrows probably lifted with that same perplexed hint of confusion.

That was when it all kind of happened at once, and I got lost in the commotion. I wasn't sure which way was up and which way was down. At least until we stopped moving anyway.

"What is he talking abou—" Frank the Tank's words were cut short by the sudden jarring motion.

The service truck kicked hard to one side. I saw my co-worker's head slam against the steering wheel. Apparently, his face is just as muscular as the rest of him, because the steering wheel and the steering wheel column collapsed against the blow. The radio flew from my hand as I sailed forward slightly in my seat, my body slamming against the passenger door. The radio crashed to the floorboard, and then we were up. And then we were down. And then we were up again. Everything around us was a blur. The service truck sounded like it was going through a meat grinder. Static from the radio filled the cab along with Ben. Ben was screaming something into the radio, but I couldn't keep my mind focused enough to make out what was being said. Amidst it all, I'm pretty sure Frank the Tank's phone rang. Boy, was his old lady going to be pissed when it went to voicemail.

The motion stopped.

I was upside down, my body pressed against the roof inside the service truck. My bones ached. My ears rang. But most importantly, I was confused. I wasn't sure what the hell was going on.

Frank the Tank grunted. When I shifted, forcing myself to see his side of the truck, I realized what had happened. We were off the road upside down in the ditch.

"You okay?" I groaned.

Frank the Tank nodded, trying to free himself from the crumpled remains of the interior of our truck. It looked like his leg was caught between the dash and what was left of the steering wheel. "Yeah… Ggrrr… you?"

"Yeah, I think. What the hell happened?"

"We got T-boned by another vehicle. Think you can get out?"

"Yeah…"

"Good. Climb out and come around to my side. I think I'm stuck."

I wiggled my way around, trying to push the passenger side door open, but it wasn't budging.

Frank the Tank's phone rang again.

"Damn it," Frank the Tank grunted, "she's going to be pissed."

The phone rang again. It sounded like it was right under me. After gliding my hand around under my weight, I found the phone. It vibrated in my hand as it rang once more.

"Here," I said, passing the phone off.

Frank took it from me and accepted the call. "Hey, honey," he said, his voice surprisingly nonchalant. "Yep. I haven't forgotten. I love you, too. No, things are going great. Just finished a job down town. Yeah… We're headed back to the shop now. Call you soon."

He hung up and pocketed the phone, but not after a few kissy kisses and smoochy smooches.

"I think my door's stuck," I said, giving it a hard shove.

From the looks of it, my door was slightly caved in, seeing as to how we were in fact upside down. It wasn't going to open, at least not for me.

"Fuck this," Frank the Tank shouted, forcing his arms up under the dashboard.

The only other time I ever heard this man raise his voice, it was on like Donkey Kong. Talk about pent-up rage. This right here is why I'm glad he's on my team. So there we were ordering us some lunch at the Taco Bell when a little old lady cut in front of him in the line. I will admit in his defense, we'd had a pretty rough day. A lot of Dees for an early day. Anyway, the little old lady cut in front of him and then had the nerve to look up at him and smile. She said something to the effect of, 'You ain't gonna do nothin', little girl.' That's one thing you don't do. You don't call Frank the Tank a girl. No sir. Frank the Tank shouted at this little old lady. Before I knew it, she was soaring through the air of the Taco Bell and went crashing through the drive through window. It was nuts. Never seen anyone throw anything that far in all my life.

"You know what to do," Frank the Tank said, tearing at the dash with all his might.

He was right. I did know what to do. "Okay, just don't kill me."

"I won't," he grunted, pushing with all he had against the dash.

With that, I began taunting my co-worker, just as that little old lady had done. "You can't tear that dash away from your legs, little girl. What are you even doing? Those sissy little arms aren't enough to set you free. You're stuck in here, and that's all there is to it. Little girl. Little girl."

I could tell Frank the Tank's blood was beginning to boil. His skin changed a shade of red. Veins began to bulge in his neck and arms. It was working. Frank the Tank grunted, and the dash began to move away from his trapped leg.

"Little girl!" I shouted. "You're a little girl!"

I could hear the plastic and metal of the dash groaning as it lifted away.

That was when I heard soft footsteps approaching us from outside. I stopped with the name calling.

"That's enough of that," a familiar voice called to us from just outside. "Don't want you pulling a hamstring."

"Hhhaa... yeah," another voice called out—the high pitched tone unmistakable. "Hemorrhoids are no fun."

Frank the Tank stopped pulling against the interior to free himself, and we both gazed upon two sets of upside down legs—the work boots of each leg firmly planted in the soft grass.

"Pat... Frank," Ben's voice crackled on the radio. "You there? Hello..."

CHAPTER TEN

Before I keep the story going, I guess it would be best to tell you a little bit about these two jack-holes that just T-boned the crap out of our service truck. The same two jack-holes that are standing in the ditch outside of our overturned truck.

The lead guy, the one with his boots in view just outside of Frank the Tank's driver side door—his name is Darrell Walker. He's a stick figure of a man with the slightest hint of meat. Keep in mind, I didn't say muscle. There is a difference. His brown, curly hair is unkempt. It points in all directions like he has just woken from one hell of a hangover. The funny thing about that is that on most days he probably has. Despite his constant nagging advances to join the A-Team of I-Corpse, Darrell is actually a pretty cool dude. He doesn't have that bed head for nothing. The dude can throw a party, and you can bet your ass that's what he's doing just about every weekend. There was a time when I considered us friends, but that was until he started singing. All day every day. The guy makes up songs all the freaking time. He sings about work and the people around him. Most of the songs are quite funny, but others can be crude or downright rude. I used to love the songs, found them entertaining. But shortly after Darrell realized he wasn't ever going to be an I-Corpse A-Team member, his songs started to strictly be about me and Frank the Tank. Needless to say that got kind of old—quick. And not to mention the time I was at one of these little parties of his and he whipped out a stack of gay porn photos. Pictures of him naked pissing into a bucket. He thought it was a joke. I thought it was disturbing. I wasn't sure if he was coming on to me or what. Creeper.

When Darrell Walker isn't around, I have made a habit of calling him Texas Walker Ranger, or Old Lady and her Walker. I'm not sure which one I like best.

So, that takes care of him.

The other guy, the high-pitched whiny voice that called out who I can't see—that's Kenneth Tate. His voice isn't naturally that high pitched. He only sounds like that when he's bitching and complaining. Sadly, I've never known him to not be crying about something. So, I've obviously never heard his voice at any other octave than high. He's a little shorter than Darrell, the Old Lady and her Walker. He always has a welding cap on. I think this is the case, because his hair is always a mess, too. But not because he parties. Because he's lazy. That's right. I said it. Lazy. Hence the whining. Nothing's ever right. For example: They could have T-boned us better. The service truck could have and should have flipped a few more times before coming to rest in the ditch. The list is endless with this guy. He has a tattoo of Crown Royal on his shoulder. I'm pretty sure he got that so his buddy Darrell Walker would think he likes parties just as much. Before all of the hate drama between the A-Team and the B-Team of I-Corpse, Kenneth and I used to hang out. Went canoeing with him once or twice. Even on a nature hike. Nice guy. But again, the end of the world and the rise of the Dees changed everyone. Back then, when we were considered friends, I used to call him

Tater Tot. I'm sure you can guess what that is. What with a name like Kenneth Tate and all. Now though, he has a new name. And that name is Puddin'. You see, there was this time when I was eating a banana and he took a snapshot of me with his phone and sent it to all his friends. "*Look at Tattoo deep throat some potassium*," he said. Everyone laughed. Everyone but me. I eventually got him back. Photoshopped his face surrounded by bulging dick bananas. What can I say? He loves pudding. Serves him right, too.

Well, there they are—Puddin' and Old lady and her Walker—standing before us, the service trucker upside down.

Their intentions up until now weren't very clear, but one thing sure as hell was.

When they T-boned us, it was damn sure on purpose.

CHAPTER ELEVEN

Puddin' laughed with his high pitched voice. "Got 'em right where we want 'em. Huh, Walker?"

Old lady and her Walker slapped his knee with one hand and nodded. "You bet," he said. "I even think I feel a song a comin'." He cleared his throat and began humming a little tune. "Frank the Tank and Pat with the tats sitting in a tree. K.I.S.S.I.N.G. First comes the truck rolling in the ditch. Then comes the A-Team getting slapped like a bitch. Tattoo's gonna cry and Frank the Tank's gonna die. You two thought you were so hot, getting all the jobs and what not. Think again, because the B-Team's back again. And we're –"

"Would you shut the hell up?" Frank the Tank shouted, cutting Old lady and her Walker's song short.

"Thank you," I said, starting to feel the blood rushing to my upside down head.

We needed to get out of this overturned service truck and take control of the situation.

I could sense Frank the Tank was thinking the same thing. He squirmed back and forth trying to free himself from his seat.

"No need trying to free yourself there, Frankie." Old lady and her Walker laughed. "We'll get you out. Won't we, Tate?"

Puddin' nodded. "Yep, we sure will! I'll be right back. Get you two out in a jiffy."

I could hear Puddin' walking away, his foot falls soft and pliable in the damp grass.

"What the hell is the matter with you two?" I shouted.

"Hey, now." Old lady and her Walker bent down so that Frank the Tank and I could see his face. He smiled. "No need to carry that sort of tone with your soon to be superior."

"What the hell are you talking about?" Frank the Tank asked, still shifting his body around to free himself.

We heard a vehicle start up. The rumble close.

"He's going to ram us again," I shouted.

Old lady and her Walker stood, his face disappearing from view. "Wait a second. Turn off the truck and come here. They don't even know."

The sound of the engine died, followed by the opening and closing of a door. The faint footsteps grew closer, and then we could hear Puddin's voice again.

"What do you mean they don't know? That's just funny."

"Yeah, sounds like we got to them before good old Ben did." Old lady and her Walker laughed louder than I ever heard him laugh at one of those parties. "You two really are in the dark on this one, aren't you?"

"What are you talking about?" I asked again.

Both of the guys from the I-Corpse B-Team stepped up to the driver's side door and knelt down so we could see both their faces. They stared at us for a long while in silence. Then Darrell, the party maniac of an Old Lady and her Walker, spilled the preverbal beans.

"I hate to say it, but it's basically like this. The old man doesn't have any more use for you. Steve is through with you. You're old news. Time to throw away the trash. Out with the old. In with the new."

"Yeah," Puddin' said. "In with the new."

Frank the Tank and I sat there upside down in the overturned service truck, dumbfounded. I just couldn't believe what I was hearing.

"It goes a little something like this." Old lady and her Walker cleared his throat. "Steve Tingbum's been running this town ever since the Dees stirred things up. The old man's got his hands into everything. The money. The food. The fuel. The housing. But most importantly... the protection. That's where I-Corpse comes in. We keep things nice and quiet on his turf. Things being nice and quiet keep the sheep of this town in line. If the people feel safe, then they do as they're told. They do as Steve tells them. They buy his food. They buy his fuel. They buy his protection. It's that simple. You see, a real business man like old Steve Tingbum can tell when going above and beyond for the client can actually hurt business. Led the clientele to think they no longer need said services. If the streets are safe again then the sheep will start to think they can leave the shepherd's borders. Do you catch my drift, big guy?"

"What does any of this have to do with us?" Frank the Tank was getting restless.

"Do I really have to spell it out for you?"

"Yeah, does he really have to spell it out for you?" Puddin' interjected.

"Shut up," Old lady and her Walker said. "I'm the one telling it here!" Darrell Walker shoved his partner, and then continued explaining things to us. "It really is quite simple, guys. You've been doing your job well. The problem is that you've been doing it too well. We need to rein it back a little bit. Let the fear creep back into the flock. Let the sheep be reminded that they need old Steve and his generous business."

"What the hell is he trying to say, Tattoo?" Frank the Tank turned toward me.

"I think he's suggesting that Steve's made an economical choice to fire us."

"You can't fire us!" Frank the Tank thrashed in his confinement.

"Oh, we ain't firing you two."

"Then what?"

"We aim to kill you!"

Puddin' and his co-worker broke out into a fit of laughter.

My skin started to boil. I couldn't believe what I was hearing. After all I had done for the man. For this company. Just like that. It was finished. It didn't make any sense. I didn't want to believe it, but I knew it was true. I gritted my teeth, my body shaking.

"Fuck this!" Frank the Tank shouted as he began prying himself free.

"You're a little girl! You have little girl arms!" I shouted, making my co-worker and friend get all the more invigorated with rage! "You little girl! You swing that dead blow hammer like a little girl!"

"Quit that!" Old lady and her Walker shouted.

It wasn't until Frank the Tank finally freed himself from the dashboard that I heard it. That familiar *click*. The A-Team wasn't accustomed to using firearms, primarily because they weren't that effective on the dead, but I knew them well. I knew the sounds they made just as well. The click of metal echoed around us as the barrel of a shotgun was hammered back ensuring the shell was in position.

"Enough playing around!" Puddin' pointed the shotgun into the cab of our service truck. "Now get out, both of you!"

CHAPTER TWELVE

Steve Tingbum sat in his office admiring the calendar on his wall. This time tomorrow, he would have two new positions open for the service crew. He pondered for a moment who he might have to fill the positions. It might be a good idea to open them to the public. Let people apply for the positions, like in the old days. A sense of something familiar. He liked that idea. Give the people a sense of normality, as if things were getting back to normal.

Proud was too strong of a word.

Or was it?

He had in fact built this city back from the ground up after everything fell apart. Sure, there were other cities like this all across America. The world even. Coming back from the rise of the Dees.

Steve just wanted to make sure that once these cities started to reconnect, he was the one that did the legwork. Pulled the strings.

He closed his eyes and leaned his head back. With a big breath of fresh air, he smiled.

Nothing like the smell of business.

CHAPTER THIRTEEN

This is the part where I got back to my relentless fear of death. Here I am with my knees in a ditch, my hands behind my head, and a shotgun pointed at my face. But before I get into my little rant about fear and death, let me explain to you our exact situation. Maybe that will help you understand why I'm feeling the way I am.

Okay, so here goes.

The I-Corpse B-Team, which is made up of Darrell Walker and Kenneth Tate (aka: Old lady and her Walker and Puddin'), have T-boned our service truck. In the process of hitting us, they managed to flip our vehicle a handful of times landing us in the ditch off the side of the road. I would like for you to consider the weight of what I'm saying here. Our service truck flipped several times landing upside down in the ditch. You realize what that means? It means a lot actually. What I'm getting at is pretty much common sense. You do realize how many bags of bodies I had stacked in the back of that truck? Severed legs, arms, and heads… and stuff.

A lot.

So, the truck flips over. Black bags scatter everywhere. Some in the road. Some in the ditch. Some on the sidewalk. Just because I spent the time cutting all these bodies up doesn't mean they are no longer harmful. That's not true at all. Not only are there now a pile of scattered body parts all around us, but they're moving. Writhing. Slithering. Some of the bags are burst open. You can see hands and knees. Heads. One corpse that I didn't cut up all that well, because I'm lazy, is crawling in the street. This crawling Dee is comprised of merely a head and a neck that is connected to a right shoulder. The shoulder nub has just enough joint bone attached that it's pivoting around in the streets. Kind of like a fish out of water when you think about it.

Blood is everywhere.

Not only is there blood everywhere, but all our tools and weapons are scattered about as well. A lot of my dynamite is in view several yards away. Shovels, rope with hooks attached to it, hazmat suits… the list can honestly go on and on. Pretty much everything in the truck came crashing out, while it rolled to a stop in the ditch. Technically we're lucky that my dynamite didn't discharge on impact.

But that's beside the point. What matters right now is right now.

Right now, Puddin', and Old lady and her Walker, are holding me and Frank the Tank at gunpoint. Both of us are on our knees in the ditch with our hands behind our heads.

So… back to the fear of death. Nothing like a shotgun to the face to bring about those types of feelings and thoughts, right?

After being in the extermination business for as long as I have, you start to realize that it's pretty much inevitable. One day you will die. Hands down. No contest. And when you do, it's Dee for you. That's right. Rotting corpse. Zombie. Walking dead. Reanimated. Ghoul. Seeking out sustenance. Eating brains and the flesh of others for no other reason that primal instinct.

I'm sorry, but that just doesn't appeal to me. I don't want any part of it. I'd rather just die and be dead. Done and over with. I don't know what would be worse. Dying in a car crash and crawling out to eat people, or dying of old age on my deathbed… lying there in those last moments realizing that this is it. This is the moment. That moment when I change over. Become that thing I hate and fear. You find yourself wondering what it would be like to become a Dee. Does it hurt? Can you feel yourself decaying? Is the hunger that drives you to feed on others painful? Do you even realize what's happening? Are you really even in there anymore? Conscious?

That's just not something I wanted to find out.

From the look in Puddin's face at the end of that shotgun barrel, I'm going to find out sooner than later.

You know, fate has a funny way of flipping the script. Changing things around when you least expect it. Wouldn't you agree?

I say that because, just when I had given in, ready to swallow a face full of buckshot, the inevitable happened.

Frank the Tank's cell phone range.

CHAPTER FOURTEEN

Frank the Tank answered his cell phone. I don't remember him pulling it from the tangled mess of the cab, but he plucked it from his front pocket just the same.

"Hey, honey… Yes, I know I missed your call." Frank the Tank's voice was calm and reassuring. "I was dealing with a customer. Yes… I haven't forgotten. On the way home, I sure will. I love you, too. I miss you."

He hung up the phone and stuffed it back into his shirt pocket, but not before saying a few smoochy-smoos and kissy-coos.

"Are you done?" Old lady and her Walker barked.

Puddin' shoved the shotgun in Frank the Tank's face.

Without even flinching, my co-worker shrugged his massive muscle toned shoulders. "Remind me to pick up milk on the way home today."

"Give me that phone!"

"I don't think so," Frank the Tank said.

Without asking, Old lady and her Walker stepped up, shoving his hand deep into my friend's shirt pocket.

Big mistake.

Before the man had a chance to even find a grip on the cell phone in Frank the Tank's shirt pocket, it was on like nobody's business.

"Only a little girl would let someone from the B-Team take away their cell phone," I muttered under my breath.

That was all it took. The fight was on.

Frank the Tank reached up, his pectorals bulging more than I have ever seen. With both hands around Old lady and her Walker's arm, his biceps pulsed with veins. Old lady and her Walker screamed. I heard bones breaking beneath the flesh of his scrawny arm.

Puddin's eyes went wide. He waved the shotgun back and forth not sure who to aim it at. Me or my partner. I stole the opportunity and lunged at him while pushing myself off my knees and onto my feet. We collided into one another with a heavy grunt. I felt the shotgun fall away as I landed atop Puddin', his back crashing hard into the wet grass. As much as I wish I had Frank the Tank's strength, I just don't. Not even close. Where me and Puddin' were a pretty even match— trading punches and rolling around—Frank the Tank was making a mess of the other guy. Between rolls and punches, I stole a glance at the other fight. It wasn't really much of a fight at all.

More like a massacre.

Frank the Tank still held Old lady and her Walker's broken arm in one hand. With his other, he pummeled the guy's crimson face over and over again. Old lady and her Walker was already limp, but Frank the Tank held him upright. Blow after earth shaking blow, fist collided with teeth. Crashed into eyes and nostrils. Made the chin fold unnaturally. With each swing of the fist, blood splashed across the ground. Frank the Tank's fist and forearm were matted with blood, loose hair, separated teeth, and pulpy chunks of face meat. Each punk was a wet *slap*. Over... and over... and over...

Darrell Walker... aka, Texas Walker Ranger and Old lady and her Walker, was dead.

My fight, on the other hand, wasn't going that great.

Puddin' punched me in the gut. I doubled over and fell to my side beside him. He sat up and punched me again. His fist came in for a third blow to the abdomen, but this time, I was ready. The punch blocked, my right knee jabbed into his chest. This tactic allowed me the leverage I needed to push him up and away.

"Frank, help!" I shouted, but he wasn't hearing me.

Frank the Tank had Old lady and her Walker to deal with. Now that Darrell Walker was dead, he was still a threat. His impaled face may have prevented the Dee from seeing, but that was about it. My partner had Old lady and her Walker's corpse pressed against the pavement of the street with the heel of his boot. With his other boot, Frank the Tank kicked. He was busy breaking leg bones and ribcage. In the street, I could see the various garbage bags from the day's catch. To my left, the truck was beside me only a few feet away still upside down. If only I could get to the truck to grab one of my dynamite sticks, or even the contents I needed to make a cocktail bomb. Something like that would surely deter Puddin' and maybe even kill him.

Speaking of Kenneth Tate, aka Puddin', formally known as Tatter tot. Where the hell was he?

I kicked him off of me—stole a glance to see how Frank the Tank was doing, and scanned the truck thinking about the need for a weapon—and now the bastard is gone.

I scanned the ditch and the street around me. Aside from Frank the Tank, Old lady and her Walker's corpse getting kicked, and the partial Dee crawling around in the street that had once been in one of my trash bags, I didn't see him anywhere.

This was my chance.

Maybe Puddin' decided to pussy out. Ran off. Probably hiding somewhere like the whiny little hit pitch baby he was.

There was no time to waste.

I jumped up, disregarded the fact my sides were sore as hell, and ran to the overturned service truck. Skimming the cab of the truck, I hoped to come across a few sticks of the good old TNT. There was none. All I found was the dead blow hammer that Frank the Tank used all the time.

"Frank!" I shouted, jutting my head back out of the cab and tossing the hammer toward him.

This time, he seemed to hear me, because he turned and caught the hammer in midair. And no, he didn't hesitate to begin using it on the Dee under his boot heel. I could hear the steady *thump—thump—thump* of the hammer as it crashed down on the undead corpse of the former B-Team 'team leader.'

What I needed to finish off Puddin' was going to be in one of the side compartments of the truck. That was of course under the assumption that it wasn't thrown into the street or ditch during the crash. I rounded the passenger side of the service truck and made my way to the back where the contents to make a cocktail bomb would be. Pulling the side door open, I stuck my head in, and began to search for what I needed. Looked like it was all there.

"Stop what you're doing!" It was Puddin's voice.

My stomach churned at the sound.

Stepping away from the service truck, I closed the side door with the readied gas bomb in my hand. If only I had something on me to light the rag hanging out of the bottle.

"Drop it!" Puddin' demanded.

Now, more than three feet away from me at the rear of the service truck, Puddin' aimed the shotgun at me. That damn shotgun. My hands began to sweat. I suddenly felt lightheaded. As much as I want to think it was the adrenaline making me feel funny, I think it was the knowing. Knowing that this was it. Knowing that this guy with the shotgun really did aim to pull the trigger. That he was going to kill me. Make me into a Dee.

I wasn't ready to die.

But... who really ever is?

The shotgun bucked in Puddin's arms. The report was very loud at such close range.

The last thing I remembered before everything went black was that heavy sensation, the push of weight as if I got shoved by a bulldozer in the stomach. The pain, although short lived, was excruciating.

CHAPTER FIFTEEN

Well, this is it. That final moment. End of the line. And I'm kind of pissed off honestly.

Nothing but utter darkness. At least the pain is gone.

Frank the Tank and I have been doing this work for a long time. Killing zombies, that is. I can remember back when it all started. Back when the company I-Corpse was formed. How Steve Tingum made the town from the ground up. How we were something the city could be proud of. Frank the Tank and I, we helped rebuild Beaumont, Texas. We really did.

And what do we get in return for that type of loyalty?

Nothing, I tell you. Disregard the sizeable paychecks, the fancy houses, and the expensive meals. Those things are a given in my book. What we should have gotten was respect. Instead, we get assassinated for doing our jobs too well.

You would think that someone like Steve would just come to us. Talk it out. Get us to take a few weeks off—paid of course. I wouldn't have seen any problem with that. The Dee problem would have started piling up again. Economical control problem solved. Simple as that.

But no... they had to send someone with a banana fetish to kill me. Shoot me in the face with a shotgun. Well, maybe not in the face, but you get the point.

It's not at all like I thought it would be... you know, becoming a Dee. I kind of figured there would be a hell of a lot more to it than just all this blackness. It's like I'm floating in the abyss or something. Kind of strange and cold.

I can't feel anything.

So... there I go again. So this... and well that... I'm not even alive, and I'm still doing it.

I wonder if it's going to be like this forever? This blackness. Just me, my thoughts, and the eternal pit of nothingness. I guess it goes to how that I had myself all worked up for nothing about becoming a Dee. There really isn't nearly as much to it as I would have—

Wait... I see a light.

Something is happening. Something is coming into focus. The world. It's coming back to me. The colors are a little bright, so it's a little hard to see, but it's coming back.

It was then I realized I was lying on my back. I can feel the wet grass under me. It's in my hands, wet and dewy. I can hear pummeling noises. A shotgun blast.

Puddin'.

After a few moments of lying there, my eyes managed to adjust to the brightness that surrounded me. Just as my eyes had adjusted, so did my hearing.

I could hear, and I could see, but I felt nothing.

The sky was blue above me. Streaks of jet streams lined the blue expanse. I thought of the conversation Frank the Tank and I had earlier that day and wondered if the jet clouds really did have anything to do with all of his.

I called out my partner's name, but all that surfaced from my lungs was a gurgled moan.

I sat up and took in my surroundings.

Puddin' was aiming the shotgun at Frank the Tank. They were both standing in the street.

Before Puddin' could either pull the trigger or reload, whichever needed to happen, Frank the Tank flung his dead blow hammer. It caught Puddin' in the shoulder. The shotgun dropped to the pavement. Frank the Tank charged.

It was at this time I started getting to my feet. It was slow going. My equilibrium felt a little off. By the time I actually got to my feet and turned toward Frank the Tank, the fight was over. Sure, while I was getting my bearings to stand, I heard a lot of commotion. Puddin' was shouting and crying like the little bitch he was. Frank the Tank's grunts and groans as he undoubtedly beat the living tar out of the guy.

But like I said... by the time I got to moving, it was over.

I staggered forward away from the service truck and into the street. For some odd reason, despite my desire to keep my hands at my sides, my arms raised toward Frank the Tank.

I think that was the moment I realized what was going on. I was dead. No doubt about it. I was staggering one slow shuffle at a time toward Frank the Tank.

Frank the Tank saw me and reached down, picking up his dead blow hammer.

With his weapon at the ready, I knew there could only be one thing coming, and I was right.

Just before the swinging commenced, I thought I saw something in my friend's eyes. Something that told me he would take care of all this. Make it all better. I imagined him cleaning things up here, and then strolling right into Ben's office. He would beat the crap out of Ben, and then find the man who did this to me, and bash his brains in with that hammer. Blow after blow after blow.

Steve Tingbum would pay.

But it wasn't Steve's face he was hitting with the hammer. It was mine.

The blunt end of the orange dead blow hammer came at me fast. The object engulfed my vision. I cried out to Frank the Tank, asking him to stop, but all that came out was an excited moan.

I felt my face cave in. I felt myself in the grass again on my back. I could see the sky. And then the orange hammer up close. Then the sky. The hammer again, so close that it blocked out my view of everything else. It was starting to get hard to see. My face felt heavy, hot, and wet.

I'm not sure how long it lasted—my co-worker bludgeoning me with a hammer to the face—but I did learn something. Eventually, the dead can die if you hit them long enough.

The last thing I heard before my consciousness was forever blotted out from the real world was one single ring.

Frank the Tank answered his phone.

"Okay, honey. I love you, too..."

EPILOGUE

Yep… here we are again with the power of narration. So, what did happened after I got my face clobbered to death by someone with biceps like that?

From what I understand, Steve's empire and the I-Corpse name are still going strong. In fact, I think Frank the Tank is still lead man for the A-Team. Still out there doing his job… but with more breaks. Boss's orders. Good for them.

As for my replacement, they apparently hired some new guy named Dillon something-or-other. Not sure what his last name was. You know what rhymes with Dillon? Mini Me, that's what. His new name is Mini Me, not because he is like I was, not even close. He actually resembles Frank the Tank in a way. That is to say, if Frank the Tank were two feet shorter, had a beer belly, and constantly talked about the Hippy Rainbow Gathering. He must have been a sunshine hipster before he got the job with I-Corpse.

No telling.

Seems kind of odd to me. Sunshine and rainbows. Rainbows and sunshine.

Sure, the world still sees its fair share of rainbows and sunshine… but not without a few zombies on the side.

The End

Read on for a bonus short story

Pussy Apocalypse
(a short bonus bizarro story)

The end of the world didn't come with a BOOM!

It didn't come with zombies like most of you would like to think.

And no, it did not come as a result of Cthulhu himself pounding through inner dimensional portals.

Nope.

None of that nonsense.

The apocalypse was started by none other than Ellen DeGenerates .

Who the hell is she to think vegan cat food was a bright idea? I tell you what... it was the dumbest idea I have ever heard of. And it was that same idea that started it all.

There I was, minding my own business, watching the DeGenerates show. So what if I'm a single man. Ain't nothing wrong with watching her show by myself. She not only looks good, but she's a lesbian. Hot lesbians are HOT, if you know what I'm sayin'.

Anyway, me and Carl—that's my cat—were watching her show. It was a typical Saturday afternoon. That's been a long time ago now, but it was when Carl and I were first introduced to HELL-O. That is Ellen's cat food. Vegan cat food. Thinking back on it now, I wouldn't doubt if they had figured out some sort of 'sound' that triggered Carl to focus so hard on the television when she started talking about that junky pet food. Come to think of it, I don't think I ever saw any cat so attentive. The way that slender cat can slide across the screen. Ellen's smiling hot lesbian face tantalizing both me and Carl.

Carl had to have it.

I didn't blame him. At least, not back then.

Hell, I had to have it, too... for Carl. I wanted to get in that chick's pants so hard.

So that day, after the DeGenerates show was over, Carl and I made a trip to the pet store. I know what you're thinking. No, I don't normally take him along, but this was somehow a special occasion. I was excited not only for Carl, but something on the television grabbed me too, the same way it did my cat. I think it was some underlying sound. Hypnotic suggestion, maybe. It was almost as if I half expected to run into Ellen at the pet store.

Sneak me in the back. Do things to Carl and me.

You know, wet things.

But it didn't happen that way at all. In fact, it played out in a way that no one would have thought possible.

The pet stores were swarming with people and their cats. Obviously, Carl and I weren't the only perverts that liked to watch her show.

The food was supposed to be healthy, nutritious, vegan.

That was where it went wrong.

Cats are carnivores in their natural habitat. They like meat. Savor the flavor of blood. I don't know about you and your cat, but Carl was always bringing me little trophies. Dead birds. Half eaten rats. Lizards with missing limbs.

But that was then.

It's not the same anymore.

Like I said, the stores were flooded with people and their cats. The pet store we went to was dishing out the

HELL-O cans so fast that I couldn't even keep up. We were at the register and checking out before I even realized my cart was slammed full of HELL-O cans. Who honestly needs that much cat food?

But I wasn't the only one lost in the trance.

Everyone around me was going through the same motions. Carts filled to the brim. Cats riding on their owner's shoulders like parrots. Hell, some people had a bunch of cats. I found out later that it wouldn't have been as bad had I had more cats. Wouldn't have been as agonizing.

As prolonged.

When we got home, Carl had to sink his maw into a can of HELL-O right away. I can't say that I blamed him then either. It took everything I had not to jump down on all fours and join him.

I had the shakes. The sweats even. Ellen was on the brain.

Carl seemed to like it. This made me happy, because I had practically cleared out my savings account on all those cans. At least it wasn't going to go to waste.

Boy, was I wrong.

The next day, Carl and I watched the DeGenerates show again. That was our weekend ritual. On this particular Sunday, all Ellen talked about was the success of HELL-O. It wasn't only good for you, but it was vegan!

Well, guess what... I hate to break it to you, but cats are not fucking vegan.

They are carnivores, point blank.

Can you imagine being fed nothing but shitty ass beans and rice? I'm not talking about for a day, or even a few days. I'm talking about all the time. Twenty-four-seven!

Come Tuesday that week, Carl quit eating the HELL-O.

He didn't want it anymore.

Fuck that shit.

This was my life savings we're talking about... right?

I guess I should have really weighed it out, then. Serves me right, I guess. Serves the whole damn world right, too.

That's right.

This wasn't just happening to me. This was worldwide, buddy.

We're talking about Ellen fucking DeGenerates here. Not some hack on the local public access. Satellite broadcasting, people! It went viral. Whatever they did to make Carl so attentive...that sub-sound, it hit everybody. If they missed that episode, they were still going out and buying this stuff just because everyone else was.

I know what you're thinking.

Not everyone has cats.

Well, by then it didn't matter. It was already too late.

So, back to the beans and rice. After the investment, I wasn't going to have Carl let it go to waste. No one was. This stuff was good for you. 'High in Nutrition' was even printed on the damn label.

"It's good for you, Carl," I said, dropping it into his bowl.

He didn't want to have anything to do with it.

It wasn't long after that when things started to really go downhill. Carl was hungry. All of them were. None of the cats wanted anything to do with the HELL-O.

Why would they? It didn't have any fucking meat in it.

Well, why didn't you let Carl just go outside and chase stuff? Let him eat a bird or something?

I tried that. A lot of people did. By the time it came to letting them outside. By the time it came to giving up on the HELL-O. All that lost money. It was too late. Carl didn't have the energy. He was getting weak. He needed substance.

He needed meat.

And I knew that.

But I just didn't know what to do.

I don't think anyone did.

And you can guess it, too. It happened when I fell asleep on the couch. And yes, it was a Saturday. And yes, I had been watching the Ellen DeGenerates marathon. Who the hell wasn't watching it?

I'm not sure what time I fell asleep.

All I do remember is the pain.

It seems to never go away now.

In the middle of my Ellen love making lesbian power dream, which was awesome I might add, Carl sank his sharp little teeth into my jugular.

I don't blame him now… now that I think about it.

He was hungry.

The pain is still just too much to bear. I am lying here bleeding out all over the couch from my torn throat. I can't call for help, because Carl did a number on my Adam's apple. Any time I try to talk it's just gurgling bubbly blood. I tried to get up, but I can't. Carl chewed on my throat for so long that I think he dug into the spine at the back of my neck or something.

I am paralyzed.

Now I can't feel it in my legs and stomach. I can't move, so I can't see, but I can feel Carl taking his time eating me. Eating my knee. Eating my stomach.

It hurts more than you can imagine. His carnivorous teeth are just so damn sharp.

At least my neck is cocked at the right angle. I can still see the television.

It's hard to listen to. The sirens, shouting, screaming, and gunfire outside in the streets of my neighborhood kind of drown out the audio, but I can still watch. And I have a pretty good guess on what is happening.

It's a rerun.

Ellen is interviewing Brad Pit.

They are laughing and slapping hands with playful banter.

I wonder when the cats staring at me through the window will figure out how to get in.

They look hungry, too.

THE OLD ONE
(SAMPLE CHAPTERS)

ONE

There was nothing special about the day leading up to that moment when his stomach ruptured. Blood splashed out around his midsection as the meaty flesh separated, sending bits of entrails and miasma all over the bed in a slopping wet heap of filth.

What spewed from his gut was an utter abomination.

It changed everything.

The day had started much like any of the other countless days for Ryan C. Perish. He was a retired old man that had been laid off from work long ago because of bad bones. The days sitting idle generally bled together. That's what made them countless.

Cool, crisp wind pushed the ocean's whitecaps against the beach and back out to the ocean. The moon set high in a cloudless sky made it unnaturally bright for such a late hour. The calm before the storm. Ryan liked it like that. Cool, calm, and quiet. He never was one to go fishing during the day. Too many problems. The pier was always overcrowded and noisy. Fishing lines got crossed. And the sun was out, which Ryan couldn't stand. At the ripe old age of 68, he couldn't tolerate the direct heat for long periods like he used to.

Topsail Beach, NC, was small family-oriented seaside island town with pristine stretches of sandy beaches. It pleased Ryan to call it home, having lived there all his life, but he was getting too old for the scene now. The paper mill was closed and everything had given way to tourism. It no longer mattered. His back was shot. There was no way for him to return to the ways of old even if the mill was still in operation.

Since retirement, he spent most of his time hanging out at the local fishermen's bar sharing stories and drinking whisky. At night, he almost always found himself in his Beavertail Phantom Water-fowling kayak. As a water-fowling kayak, the Phantom was specifically built to overcome the challenges often found when hunting out of smooth-bottomed, conventional kayaks. The twin-hull, catamaran-style bottom provided a stable platform to support the additional weight of hunting gear. Hunting wasn't the reason why he owned the boat. He wasn't a hunter. Didn't even own a gun. He hated firearms with a passion. His younger brother had been killed by a handgun. He didn't like to go near them.

He bought a Beavertail Phantom because of its stability. He could sit and relax, even when the waves were somewhat choppy, even while tied off under the pier.

That night, the waves were nonexistent. The water was as flat as flat could be. The only occasional sounds were splashes of fish feeding on top-water insects. The smell of sea salt and the gentle breeze eased his internal pains.

Ryan took a deep breath and exhaled a sigh of relief as he leaned back in the kayak to get more comfortable. He had been tied off at the far end of the pier for the last two hours just relaxing and casting his line. He hadn't caught anything yet, not even a single bite, but it didn't matter.

The silence, smell, the full moon, and the view of an endless black were enough for him to enjoy the night.

He reached into his coat pocket and pulled out a half empty flask of bourbon. He unscrewed the top, took a long swig, and sucked air in through his teeth. The spirits burned going down. No matter how much he drank, he never could get used to it. His chest felt warm as the alcohol settled in his stomach. Satisfied, he took one more quick sip, sloshed it around in his mouth, and put the flask back into hiding.

Despite what tourists happening upon him might have thought, Ryan wasn't the town drunk that spent most of his nights fishing. Sure, he fished a lot, but he wasn't a drunk. He drank, but wasn't the stereotypical overbearing bum. He had his own place on the edge of town. Like all of his possessions, it was paid for. He had enough money saved up from working at the mill to not burden anyone. At least, he felt like he wasn't a burden on anyone. He sure as hell hoped he wasn't. Sure, Trent and Tina, his neighbors, helped him with his grocery shopping, but that wasn't because he was feeble. It wasn't like he needed help getting in and out of the shower or cleaning house. He just didn't like to shop alone. Heather had always been the one to do that, but just like the old paper mill, she went before her time.

Ryan missed her deeply. Everything about her. Her scent. Her sweet endearing laugh. The way one dimple formed on the left side of her cheek when she smiled.

If there was any one thing worse than guns, it was cancer.

Cancer had taken his wife.

Ryan smiled. A lone tear fell from his right eye. It wasn't from sadness or loneliness. No, he wasn't one to suffer from much of that. His tear was shed out of joy. He had loved Heather more than anything in the world. And despite the hand in life that had been dealt, he was thankful that his mind was still in working order, unlike some of the others his age back at the bar. At least, he was lucky enough to recall the memories of the life he and Heather shared. See her image in his mind. It was as if she were sitting in the kayak with him. The cool ocean draft lightly blew across his neck and tickled the hairs on his skin. For a moment, it reminded him of her tender touch.

That was one of the main reasons he fished so much. It always made him think of her.

The fishing rod suddenly jerked in his hand, breaking him from the spell of the past.

He had a bite.

"Got you now," he whispered.

He tightened his grip on the rod and scanned the dark trying to locate the end of the line. His eyes weren't what they used to be. The fish tugged again and he found what he was looking for. The small red and white float dunked under the water and resurfaced.

He smiled.

"Looks like another lucky night, Heather." He yanked the rod a few times to set the hook and watched the water.

The reel began to unwind sounding like a bug in distress. He hoped he snagged a big one. Another hard yank locked the reel.

"The Big kings must still be in." He heaved, testing the resolve of his catch.

If it was a Big king, then there was about to a bit of a fight. The largest one he had ever caught was 48 lbs. Ryan had spent most of the week bottom fishing. VA mullet hit best on bloodworms, but he managed to catch a few spots, some puppy drum, flounder, and trout during the week, but that was it. With the cooler weather starting to come in, the overall conditions for fishing had started to improve.

Ryan tugged.

The catch tugged back. The fight began.

He stood in the kayak like he had done countless times before. The wide berth the small boat provided kept it from tipping over. In truth, he wasn't even sure why it was called a kayak. It really didn't even look like one to him. He craned his head to the right, checking the rope's knot he had tied to the pier. It was still tight. Satisfied, he tugged hard, lifting the fishing pole up over his head, reeling it in with everything he had. Each breath he took strained against his brittle old lungs.

Come on, old man, you got this, he thought. He gave the rod slack for a second and pulled back to gain the advantage. We ain't lettin' this one get away. His arm muscles, despite their old age, tightened. Veins bulged in his neck. There wasn't much of the fishing line left. Whatever he had on the other end of that hook wasn't much further from the surface.

Ryan jumped with a twinge of fright when the fish broke the water's surface even though he was expecting it. Water splashed across his legs into the boat. The Big king's head flailed violently against the hook as he tried to pull it in.

"Dang… you sure are a big'n," Ryan said, trying to catch his breath.

The fish's scales glistened against the moonlight as it slid over the kayak's side into the boat. Ryan sat down to rest, setting the rod in its holster to free his hands to keep the large fish from flopping out.

"Eh?" he cringed. The was hook stuck out of the fish's eye.

Ryan loved fishing. Didn't mind the smell. Didn't mind the sticky fingers from handling the live bait. But this was a little much. Removing the hook was the part he never got used to. He never was one for scaling and cleaning. He always just put his catch on ice and got the local butcher to deal with it the next morning. So what if it cost a couple bucks. To him, any money was worth not having to stick his hands down the damn thing's mouth and yank out entrails.

Ick…

Now, he knew better than to roll his eyes and play fingertip tug with the hook when he was around some of the other roughnecks that fished. And if any of them caught wind of it, he knew good and well that it would spread like wildfire back at the bar. It didn't matter. It was late. No one was around. At least, he thought no one was around. He took one reassuring glance to either side anyway, feeling silly. Unless Earl Harper, one of his buds from the bar, could walk on water and didn't have to be at work in the morning, there was no reason to think anyone would see him playing skittish with the fishing hook.

He might have been a little silly about the gore, but Ryan wasn't dumb. With his left hand still holding the flailing fish to the floor of the kayak, he reached into his pants pocket and retrieved his pocket knife.

"Sorry 'bout this, pal," Ryan said, stabbing the fish in the area where its heart should have been, "but I don't need to get my hand hooked. No, sir. That wouldn't be any good."

Ryan waited a moment. The fish's squirming subsided to nothing more than labored gasps for air.

He heard a bird's wings flap close by overhead. Probably taking perch at the top of the pier waiting for scraps. That was another one of the reasons Ryan hated fishing during the day. The birds were out of control. It would never fail. Someone always got shit on by those stupid rats with wings. Between the kids feeding the damn things and the idiots that felt the need to gut their fish right then and there, the birds overran the place. The dumb thing was probably on the railing overhead waiting for a hand out. If there was anything worse than the birds, it was a bum, and these birds were both.

He didn't bother looking up. With his right hand applying pressure, the knife still lodged in the thing's heart, he reached for the hook with his free hand.

"Let's get this over with." Ryan gritted his teeth, the cold wet hook grasped between two fingers. "Got to admit though, good catch. Don't you think, Heather?"

Just pull the damn thing out, he thought, as if it were his Heather telling him somehow. He knew better. Old habits were hard to break, and talking to her wasn't one he was looking to be giving up.

Ryan closed his eyes and took a deep breath.

He pulled hard on the hook. There was no point in trying to pry the hook out, leaving the fish's flap trap intact. When he brought it in to get cleaned, they were going to chop the head off anyway. The sound of flesh tearing reached his ears. When he looked down, the hook was in his hand. The dead creature's maw had been nearly torn clean off. Chunks of skin and meat dangled from the hook. Blood smearing his thumb and pointer finger made him instinctively reach over into the water to rinse his hand before setting the hook aside.

Ryan's scream was cut short. A watery splash took its place.

Something grabbed his hand from within the drink. He was overboard and in the water before he realized what the hell was happening.

The cold rushed over his body as his mind struggled to realize he had been pulled from the boat.

He gasped for air. It felt like two hands squeezed each of his lungs as tight as they could. His mind swirled and his eyes burned against the salty blackness. He fought against the water around him, trying to decide which way was up. Both of his hands were free and whatever had pulled him in wasn't there now.

Panic set in.

Whatever it was, it was probably still close by. His heart raced. It pounded against his chest with a fierce trembling, and hurt just as bad as his lungs. His mind went white. Heather was there standing before him. She was wearing a long, flowing white robe. Against the white around her, it was almost hard to make out anything else except her face, hands, and feet. She glistened like an angel full of light and pure love. His heart swelled with peace despite the situation, despite whatever the hell had pulled him from the boat. He reached out trying to take her hand. Embrace the light. Finally be with her for eternity. God, he wanted that more than anything. To finally be able to hold her in his arms after all those years alone. He tried to tell her he loved her and missed her. Wished she was still with him. But he couldn't talk. She reached up putting a cold finger on his lips. It felt coarse and slimy. No matter. It was good to feel her touch after all that time. She told him it was going to be okay. His time wasn't over yet. She had a bigger purpose for him. She needed him to live. There were other things to do. She reached out, pulling him into her and kissed him on the lips. Ryan felt a tear form in the corner of his eye despite the fact that he knew he was still under water. Something slammed violently in the back of his throat and went down hard. He felt sick. The reality that he couldn't breathe was finally setting in. His stomach churned, and then, Heather's beautiful face changed into something hideous. And like that, she was gone. The blackness and his stinging eyes returned. Just when his limbs were about to go limp and his mind wavering into a darker place, Ryan felt the ocean floor at his feet.

He kicked against it as hard as he could and rushed to the water's surface.

He broke to the surface and gasped for air. Waves of numbing coldness washed over his entire body. Pain flooded his lungs, as if the air entering was unexpected.

He lunged forward, somehow sitting up in bed. Had it all been a bad dream?

His mind was clouded and confused. Whose bed was he lying in? He had never seen this room before in his life. The clothes he had been wearing were folded neatly on a nightstand next to him. They were pressed and dry. That was when he realized he wasn't wearing anything. He lifted the blanket and found that he was bare down to his skivvies. He took in the room, hoping for the slightest hint as to where he was. A photo on the wall. A familiar friend sitting in a chair. There was nothing. The room was empty. Just him, the nightstand, and the bed. A small wooden Crucifix hung on the wall above the bed. That was it.

He remembered the fishhook. He remembered falling in the water. Or did he get pulled in? He remembered seeing his love, Heather. She had said something to him, but what it was, he couldn't remember. It was important. That much he knew.

"Hell…ooo?" Ryan called out, his throat hoarse. "Hello? Is someone there?"

"He's awake," someone called out from another room.

A moment later, the last person Ryan expected to see stepped in view.

"Hey, Perish," Paul Stellie said, stepping in the doorway with a wide smile.

"Hey, buddy," Ryan replied, clearing his still sore throat.

Paul was about 19 years old. Great kid, a bag boy at the local farmers market on the other side of town. Pretty much everybody knew everybody on the island. Like most teenagers, he was going through phases, but that was nothing. He worked hard, played hard, and rarely got into trouble. Ryan had known him since he was just a small pup. It had always amazed the old man to watch him grown up into the young adult he was. They would chat it up at the farmers market on the occasions Paul had helped him with his groceries to the car.

Paul was into something called the Facebook, or the Bookface. Ryan wasn't sure. Maybe it was some new band the kids were into these days. Other than that, he was currently saving most of the money he made from being a bagboy for a set of wheels. The way Paul put it, 'I'm never going to get a girlfriend being driven around by my mom all the time.' They both laughed about that, because it was true. Ryan enjoyed their chats. Beyond the small talk, it never went anywhere else. But that was to be expected. What teenager wanted to be seen being friends with an old lonely man like Ryan?

Paul's mom, Rose Stellie, was a widow. Unlike cancer that had taken his Heather away, Mr. Stellie had been taken from this life by a drunk driver a few years back. Surprisingly, Paul and his mother had taken it a lot better than the rest of town had expected them to. Ryan wasn't sure what she did for a living. Other than being a little on the sad side, she was a really kindhearted lady.

"Had us sacred, man. Glad to see you came around." Paul grinned, rubbing the stubble on his chin.

"Where are we?" He knew it was silly to ask. They were at Paul's house. That was the logical answer. But when he opened his mouth that was what came out.

"My casa-su-casa. You're in the spare bedroom," Rose Stellie said, stepping past Paul with a glass of water. "Here—drink this."

"Thanks," Ryan said, sitting back against the headboard and looking down to make sure he was covered up. He took a big gulp from the glass and said, "What happened?"

"Dude, I'll tell you what happened," Paul said, his voice high pitched with excitement. "You almost died. That's what. Me and Chels…" He cleared his throat and started over. His mom glared at him. "I mean me and Chelsea was walking up and down the beach. Just when we were about to head up onto the pier, I heard something splash in the water. That was when I spotted your boat tied off at the far end."

Ryan's mind flashed to that moment when his hand went into the water.

"But you weren't on the boat," Rose spoke up. "You were lucky, Mr. Perish. Had Paul and Chelsea," she rolled her eyes at her son, "not been there you would have drowned."

"Yeah, dude." Paul smiled, his shoulders straight with pride. "Once I got to the shoreline, Bro, you popped up gasping for air. I jumped in after you, dude. Good thing the tide wasn't in. I don't know that I would'a been able to pull you in by myself."

Thanks, Paul." Ryan nodded, and then looked down at the folded clothing on the nightstand. "How long have—"

"You were out for nearly a whole day," Rose said, cutting him off. "It's seven o'clock and the sun's already gone down. I'm sure you could use something to eat. How does something light sound."

"That would be great," Ryan said, taking another sip from his glass of water.

Rose nodded and turned away leaving Paul and Ryan to themselves.

"She'll be back in a second." The teenager said. "We had some soup already on the stove."

"That's nice." Ryan smiled, ignoring the tense feeling in his stomach. "So, who is this Chelsea girl? I thought you weren't having any luck with the ladies what with not having a car to call your own."

"Yeah. Well, uh," Paul said, flustered. Running his fingers through his sandy-brown hair, he said, "Well, my Mom don't much care for her, but what does she know? I think she…"

Ryan tried listening to the boy as he talked about this girl—obviously smitten, but he couldn't focus. His stomach started cramping and it felt like it was going to burst from the seams at any moment. Something was wrong. It was almost as if he was experiencing a severe kidney infection. He grabbed at his side trying to breathe. He stretched in the bed trying to make the pain go away. It was only getting worse. The pain rapidly grew so harsh that his vision started to blur.

"I…" That was the last word Ryan C. Perish had the chance to utter.

His body convulsed in a fit of agony.

"Oh, my God!" Rose shouted, stepping into the room and nearly dropping the bowl of soup in her hand. Setting it on the nightstand, she shouted at Paul to go call for help.

Before Paul could turn around and make his way out of the room, Ryan's midsection exploded. With a painful gurgling grunt, his stomach ruptured in a firework display of red and white. Blood sprayed across his body all over the bed. His intestines slapped wet in his lap. Blood ran down his chin from his open mouth, his eyes soulless and vacant. Chunks of meat splashed across the wall, bits of it falling to the floor.

Rose screamed.

Ryan C. Perish was dead.

The tentacle-like things that squirmed out from inside the old man's corpse were on Rose and her son before either of them could comprehend what was happening.

TWO

Max Willgood smiled, poking his head past the blinds of the window in his den.

"Looks like it's gonna start raining soon," he said, looking out toward his neighbor's house.

"What'd the weather channel say, dear?" his wife Hanna asked, from behind her needlepoint project.

"Not sure. Didn't catch the weather today," he replied, not taking his eyes away from the window.

The sky outside started to grow bleaker by the minute. He was right. Thick and menacing clouds rolled in. A faint grumble of thunder echoed off in the distance, followed by a sudden flash of bright white.

"Hmmm…" He shook his head. "When it rains, it pours."

"Would you get away from that window already?" Hanna insisted. "You're making me anxious. It's the first day of vacation and you're already restless. Now, come sit down. Let's find something to watch on TV."

"I'm not the one who wanted to take vacation," Max muttered. "I would'a been just fine with a payout. We could use the money."

Hanna didn't say anything. She never did. She just shrugged and went back to her embroidery. They had been married for well over ten years now. Knew each other inside and out. Most people married for that length of time thought it was cool to finish one another's sentences. Hell, they could finish each other's thoughts. They could just look at one another and know what they were going to say. When they first moved to Topsail Beach about 5 years ago, Max had gotten a job as an auto mechanic at one of the local shops. He loved working with his hands, so he enjoyed the job. It had actually been Hanna's idea for them to make the move. The economy had been pretty rough up north and they both hated the cold weather. And since Max was naturally high strung, Topsail Beach seemed like the perfect place to relocate. Stress-free living was what they needed. Small, family oriented. Everybody knew everybody. They liked that quality. Before they actually committed to the move, Max managed to lock the job at the local repair shop. Don's Automotive. Because of that, the deal was sealed. Wasn't the greatest in pay, but it worked. Having gotten married early on at the ripe old age of 19, both he and Hanna were only 29, going on 30. Hanna was the one closer to 30 by about two months, but if you had asked, she would deny it. She was currently between jobs which was why Max would have preferred the check over the days off. But, with the use it or lose it policy in effect, he took it. He didn't like it. He didn't like sitting idle and he knew Hanna could tell. Being at home all day was eating at him. She just smiled and shook her head some more, then went back to threading her needle.

A loud roar grumbled outside suggesting the rain would soon fall.

"Looks like it's about to start getting pretty nasty." Max stepped away from the window, scratched the thick mustache under his bulbous nose and sat down next to Hanna in his recliner. "And no… I don't plan on shaving it any time soon, dear."

"But I don't like it," she said, rolling her eyes at him. "It tickles my face when we kiss."

"You're just going to have to get used to it." Max said, licking at the mustache with his lips. He grabbed the remote to the TV and turned it on. Finding the weather channel, he nodded. "You know good and well that if I'm to be the best mechanic this side of the island I need to look the part."

She chuckled.

He definitely looked the part. Too well in fact.

His scruffy jet black hair was short and somehow always a mess. His monster of a mustache just as thick, and just as dark, aside for the one small patch of gray hairs under his left nostril. When the discolored hairs had first started to show, Hanna insisted he not pluck them out. That it gave him character. He thought it was silly, but kept them anyway. Hanna hated his mustache and if there was one thing she did like about it, he sure as hell wasn't going to get rid of that.

"So, what's this one going to be?" Max leaned up from his chair trying to sneak a peek at Hanna's needlepoint.

She pulled it up to keep him from seeing it. "You know you can't look until I'm finished."

When they first bought the house, they came across tons of yarn and unfinished yarn art pieces in the attic. They must have been left by the previous owners. Hanna had never been into needlepoint before then, but instantly fell in love with it. Surprisingly, she had a knack for it. Before long, she was spitting out a new piece every couple of weeks. The wall the flat screen television set on was lined from one end to the other with pieces she had completed. Mushroom embroideries, houses, owls, cats, all of them hand embroidered with care. She was actually getting really good at it. Before long, there wouldn't be any more room on that wall for her creations and her art would be encroaching on the other wall space that had been designated for family photos.

Max didn't mind. It made her happy and she really did seem to enjoy it.

He thumbed the volume on the remote, the commercials finally giving way to the weather.

"The hurricane season has officially kicked off. It's going to be another active season with Tropical storm Faye stirring up trouble in the Atlantic off the coast of North Carolina," the weatherman on TV was saying. "Last year's season had 19 named storms, 10 category 1 hurricanes and 1 major category 4 hurricane. From 1995 to 2011, the Atlantic has averaged 15 named storms, 8 hurricanes and 4 major hurricanes. This is not to be taken lightly and preparations have been taken as local citizens are gearing up for another bumpy year. With maximum sustained winds suggested to reach up to 70 mph when Faye reaches landfall, the

Tropical storm could very well develop into a hurricane by daybreak. It is however expected to reduce its…"

"Preparations?" Max scoffed, drowning the television out. "I didn't even know we had a storm headed this way, did you?"

"Nope." Hanna smiled, her pearly whites just above the embroidery she was working on. "I thought I heard Becky talking to someone about the weather when I stopped by the store to get some milk and eggs this morning. But I didn't notice anybody rushing to get supplies or anything."

"Hmm…" Max shrugged. "That's crazy. Hopefully, it doesn't turn out to be a big one. Remember last year when the bridge out of Surf City got flooded out? That sucked."

"Yep," Hanna agreed, her hands still steady at work on the yarn art.

The island only had one way to the mainland other than by boat, and that was to drive all the way through Surf City on the other side of town and hit the bridge onto the mainland. It never failed. When there was an evacuation, you could forget trying the bridge. It was always congested as hell.

"You think we should go to the store and stock up on stuff just in case?"

"It wouldn't hurt." Hanna set the embroidery aside then stood to her feet. "I'm going to go get something to drink. You want anything?"

Max nodded.

Just when she was about to step out of the room and into the kitchen, she turned back and said, "And no peeking!"

Max laughed and she stepped out of the room. Sure enough, he snuck a glance at what she had been working on for well over a week. It was embroidery of some of the characters from The Muppets. The only one he recognized was the frog and the one named Ms. Piggy.

"You better not be peeking!" Max heard Hanna call out from the kitchen.

It made him smile.

Sitting there waiting on his wife to return, he started flipping the channels to find a movie for the two of them to watch. When he listened closely enough, he could hear the faint sound of rain outside. It had already started coming down.

Gonna be another great hurricane season, he thought. Always got to trade one thing for another. Guess the rain is better than the snow.

A sudden crash outside startled Max. At first, he brushed it off as the storm got closer, but it didn't sound like thunder. It sounded more like something was out in the yard. He turned down the television and sat there for a second listening. He could hear the rain beating against the roof. It was coming down harder than he thought. Thunder bellowed out in a low drone and faded off. He started to turn the volume back up, but then he heard it again. Something metallic sounding rattled in the yard. He could hear it like it was right on top of him. He thought about it for a second. The trash did get picked up tomorrow and Hanna had taken the trash out earlier. Maybe it was a stray dog trying to dig through the trash for scraps.

His curiosity sparked, Max climbed out of the recliner and went to the door to take a look.

He peered through the peep hole in the door and flicked the switch for the porch light. The sudden harsh light illuminated the porch and beyond. Sure enough, one of the trashcans out by the road had been knocked over, but there was nothing around. No sign of an animal or anything. He knew that the weather said it was going to get bad, but there was no way the wind had blown it over. He thought of going outside to pick up the toppled can, but really didn't want to with the rain coming down like it was. His eyes craned left and right, checking the tree line through the peep hole. None of the trees seemed to be blowing out of control… yet.

"What'cha doing?"

Max jumped, goose-bumps sliding up his arms and across the back of his neck. When he turned around, Hanna waited with a glass of iced tea. A single slice of lime floated at the top of the ice, just how Max liked it.

"Thanks, honey," he said, shaking his head and taking the drink.

"Scared much?" She asked, giggling as she walked across the living room to take a seat back at her embroidery station.

"Something tipped one of the trash can's over." He insisted, trying to justify the startle.

Hanna just laughed.

He didn't bother trying to explain it. To give reason to the fright would only ensure her that he had been gotten good, and he didn't need that. She wouldn't let him live that one down for a long time. Either that or until he got her back.

He just shrugged it off, giving her due credit for the scare and took a seat back in the recliner. He would go out and pick the trash up when the rains slowed some. He took a few sips of tea and found something to watch on TV. Dexter's Laboratory. So what if he was 30 years old. You were never too old for cartoons. And since Boomerang started showing it instead of Cartoon Network, he was starting to feel his age. Oh well… It was one of the episodes where DeeDee was messing around in his lab when she shouldn't. Come to think of it, that was just about every episode.

They sat there for a while, Max laughing at Dexter getting mad at his sister, and Hanna lost in the world of embroidery.

When the knock at the door broke the silent comfort, this time it was Hanna that jumped. Only it was less like a knock and more like a thump. Something heavy had just slammed against their front door. Both Max and Hanna stared at one another for a moment. Then it happened again. The violent thud made Max turn off the television and jump to his feet.

"What is it?" Hanna whimpered, setting her needlepoint stuff to the side.

"No idea, love." Max lifted a finger to suggest she hang tight for a second. He cautiously walked to the door and looked through the peephole. "It's Rose and her son, Paul, from across the street."

"Oh…" Hanna smiled, the tension instantly lifted. "She said she was going to bring some soup over later."

"Why does she always cook so damn much?" Max rolled his eyes. "That kid of hers ain't eating, so why does she feel the need to make us eat it?"

"She's just trying to be nice," Hanna said, very matter-of-factly. "And besides, cut her some slack. You know things have been tough on her since the accident. Now, invite them in already."

"Yeah…" Max agreed, turning the doorknob and opening the door. "Hey, Ro—

Rose lunged forward, forcing the door to slam hard into Max. He fell back trying to catch himself, his footing off balance. He tumbled hard to the floor hitting his back against the wall.

Hanna screamed.

When Max looked up, puzzled by what was happening, his mouth dropped open in disbelief. Hanna was being attacked… attacked by Ms. Rose Stellie. Hanna fought against her attacker. Rose thrashed violently, hissing and grunting with rage. That was when Max noticed the blood. Rose was covered in it. Before he had the chance to stand to his feet and defend his wife, Paul stepped through the doorway and locked eyes with him. The teenager's hands were covered in blood. And red ran down from a gaping hole in his throat where his Adam 's apple should have been. The cavity was dark in the center and seeped puss and plasma, covering his shirt with blood.

Thunder boomed from outside.

"Oh, my God…" That was all Max was able to mutter before the Farmers Market bag boy charged at him with both hands out ready to kill.

Max lifted his legs and kicked as hard as he could, using the wall at his back as leverage. Paul staggered backward. The momentary distance forced Max to action. He stood on his feet trying to calm the teen. Paul didn't respond to his calming tone. Just before the kid charged him again, Max looked over the young man's shoulder across the living room. Hanna was still in trouble. Rose was on top of her, his wife pinned between the crazed neighbor and the recliner she had been sitting in before.

Paul hissed, spitting bloody saliva across the carpet, and leapt toward Max.

This time, the auto-repair man was ready. He sidestepped just in time, grabbing the teen by the arm. Using Paul's momentum, Max shoved him as hard as he could right into the wall. Paul slammed into it hard. The bone shattering thump sent chills down Max's spine. When Paul turned around to face Max again, the wall where his face had hit was smeared with crimson. The bag-boy hissed again, his wide maw showing missing teeth. When Max sidestepped the second attack by Paul, out of the corner of his eye, he saw teeth actually imbedded into the wall.

"What the fuck is happening?" Max screamed, shoving Paul headlong into the flat screen TV. Dexter's Laboratory was instantly obliterated when Paul's head went through the screen and into the wall on the other side. With his head still shoulder deep in the television, Paul fell limp right there, his knees hitting the carpet and his arms flaccid.

Max stood there for a moment taking it all in. This couldn't be really happening. He was sitting in the recliner having a crazy day-dream; the result of not wanting to take the vacation work forced him to take. But he wasn't snapping out of it. Not, this was real. He heard the slurping grunts and gurgles. It forced him to look up. When he did, the sight before him made his chest drop into his feet. He felt woozy and lightheaded. Rose was leaning over Hanna. There was blood everywhere. Hanna wasn't moving. Her eyes were wide and vacant.

"What have you done?" Max breathed, his words choked out by disbelief.

Rose stopped what she was doing to Hanna and looked up at him. Max swallowed hard, frozen in fear. Rose was covered in blood. Hanna's blood. When she shifted her weight to look up at him, he caught a glimpse of what was happening. She had blood all over her hands. The meat dangling from her lips as she snarled at him fell to the carpet. It was Hanna's meat. Rose was eating her!

Slowly, Rose stood up from Hanna's unmoving body and locked eyes with Max. Her eyes were mad with rage. Chunks of flesh fell from her hands as she raised them at him. The wet slap the meat made when it hit the carpet made Max's stomach churn.

"Rose…" Max pleaded, his voice brittle. "Why?"

Rose roared an animalistic grunt and charged at him.

She hit him head on and Max stumbled backward. Her teeth chomped violently over and over again. As they collided together, it was like clamping vices that rang in Max's ears. Still back peddling, he held her head at bay with his hand held at her throat. His hand felt wet and warm against the gaping cavity where her throat should be. That was when he realized her neck was the same as Paul's. He stole a glance at Paul lying motionless on the floor, his head still in the TV.

Fear flooded Max's mind as he wrestled with his neighbor, who was just supposed to be bringing some soup over. What the hell was going on? He shoved her hard, providing distance between them. Not knowing what to do, he reached up on the wall and yanked down a framed photo he and Hanna had taken the last time they had gone to Disney World. It had been just before the big move to NC. In the photo, Hana was getting kissed by Goofy and Max was acting shocked. It had turned out to be a cute photo. When the frame came down, it came down hard. He swung with everything he had. Glass shattered across Ms. Stellie's head. The frame came apart in his hands and Rose fell back from him, falling to the floor.

That was his chance.

He turned to head toward the kitchen, but not before taking once last look at Hanna. She was breathing. She was still alive.

A loud thud drew his attention to the front door. The front door was still wide open. The rain outside was getting so rough that the wind was forcing into the doorway. The carpet was becoming soaked with each droplet that entered, landing on the carpet. Old man Ryan C. Perish was shambling toward the door and had stumbled to his knees trying to get through the door. The old man was soaking wet, but something was wrong with him. He was dead. He had to be. His skin was pale and was wearing nothing but his underwear. He was covered in blood from head to toe, the rain not doing much to wash it off his clammy body. But that wasn't what was wrong. It wasn't the hole in his throat like Rose and Paul. No, he didn't have a hole in his throat. He had a fucking hole the size of a damn basketball where his stomach should have been. His insides had spilled out. Chunks of meat and a link of intestine dangled down to his knees from the globular tumor of a hole. Unlike Rose and Paul, he didn't charge forward. He was still at the door struggling to maintain balance while he entered the house.

"What the fuck!" Max screamed.

From his peripheral he saw Rose starting to get back up. He craned his neck and stole a glance at Hanna. He had to do something.

He turned and ran toward the kitchen.

I need something. Hanna needs me. He panted, racing into the kitchen while trying to make sense of it all. The bedroom!

Three Christmases ago, Hanna's father had given him a revolver. He wasn't much of a gun person. In fact, he hadn't even taken the time to get familiarized with the revolver. He'd never shot it before. Even still, it was in the bedroom, probably still sitting in the box it had been wrapped in and hidden in the back of the closet collecting dust. He rounded the corner passing through the kitchen. Hanna had left the pitcher of tea out. She did that a lot and would later complain as if Max had been the one to leave it out.

In the bedroom, he closed the door and darted to the closet. Shoving clothing aside, he sifted through the boxes on the floor among the plethora of shoes Hanna owned but never wore.

"Come on… come on… I know you're in here."

It wasn't.

"Shit…" He panicked. "The bed!"

He turned, falling flat on the floor and digging under the bed. The box was there. When he pulled it out, tearing it open, he heard Rose hunting for him. It was as if she were some type of wild animal. He cradled the revolver and gritted his teeth, trying to work the small box of bullets open. The box fell open, the bullets scattering across the carpet.

The loud crash at the door startled him.

"Fuck… fuck… fuck…" He gasped, falling to his knees and scooping bullets into his hand.

The door shook pugnaciously, Rose's pounding relentless. It was a surprise the door didn't come down with her giving it hell like that.

With his nerves shot, he struggled to force the bullets into the revolver. It was as if the bullets were too thick to go in the little holes. Finally, one slid into place… and then another, and another. With six bullets chambered, he stood to his feet and stuffed what bullets were left in his front pocket. He gritted his teeth, hoping like hell that the gun would fire. It hadn't been oiled or maintained; not once.

He aimed the gun at the shaking door. Grunts and hissing bellowed out from the other side.

Max thought of Hanna lying there dying in the living room. "Why are you doing this, Rose?" He started to cry. "Have you gone mad?"

Of course she had. She burst down his damn door and starting eating his wife!

With his finger on the trigger, he tried to steady his hands but couldn't. Whether it was the fear of the fact he wasn't ever really comfortable with guns, it didn't matter. He needed to pull it together. The thought of Hanna surfaced again and something came over him. His hands quit shaking and his nerves became more focused. The sickness trying to overtake his stomach subsided and he knew what he needed to do.

Funny thing, when you think about it.

Although Hanna loved watching horror movies, Max never really could stomach them. Blood, guts and violence just weren't his cup of tea. Even if they came with a lime to top it off. But when you are faced with real life, it goes to show that you can do just about anything when forced in a corner. The love of your life is in danger and needs medical attention and the only thing between you and getting her that help is a crazy bitch that can't cook to save her life. Then there was Ryan and Paul. He didn't even want to think about Ryan, the town drunk. Someone walking around with that big of a hole in them just wasn't plausible. And Paul… what he had done to Paul. He could have killed him. And if that's what it was going to come down to, then so be it. If death was what stood between him and saving Hanna, well... he thought the—

The door blew open, Rose tearing it from its hinges.

Max screamed, simultaneously squeezing the trigger for the first time ever.

Rose plummeted toward him. The revolver jolted in his firm grip. Although he was ready for the recoil, it burned his palms. Smoke fluttered from the barrel and Max watched the bullet do its damage.

It tore the flesh form her shoulder like melted butter. The blood sprayed from the exit wound across the wall and Rose didn't even flinch. She just kept coming.

Max screamed again and felt bile start to rise in his throat. He squeezed the trigger again and just when Rose was about to grab hold, the bullet caught her in the left eye. Her eye socket exploded, slashing miasma and blood across Max's face and chest. She fell limp to the floor at his feet. All the while, Max could hear the bullet rattling around in her skull, turning her brain into potted meat.

Max tried to take a breath and vomited instead. His gut tightened like a metal vice and the dinner Hanna had cooked earlier along with the iced tea flowed out like a river all over Rose's corpse.

The smell and the sight of her at his feet made his stomach churn even more. His knees started to buckle, but he forced his body to move. Hanna was in trouble. His mind was so set on helping her that he completely forgot about old man Perish.

Leaving the bedroom and rounding the hallway corner into the kitchen, he almost ran right into the old drunk's arms. The old man groaned, startling Max to attention. He sidestepped and lifted the barrel of the gun against his head. Just when the old man started to shift his weight to advance, Max pulled the trigger. The loud report of the gun reverberated off the tile floor. Max's ears rang as he watched the old man's brain explode out the back side of his head.

Max didn't even stop to look or think. There would be time for that later. Hanna needed him.

He was in the living room and at her side within seconds. Ignoring the wide open front door and the mess of bodies scattered across his home, he cradled her in his arms.

"It's going to be okay, honey." He wiped blood from her face. "I'm going to get help."

She was cold and she wasn't breathing.

Her eyes were lifeless and staring at nothing.

Emotion overwhelmed him like a flood as he pulled her into himself and cried.

Hanna was dead, her throat and face gushing blood where Rose had taken out chunks with her teeth.

He sat there covered in muck and blood, holding her, crying and confused.

When Paul's stomach started to make noise, Max was too lost in everything to notice. Hanna needed him and he had failed.

The sound was wet like squishing gelatin between your fingers.

Paul Stellie's stomach split open, spilling out more than a dozen writhing things from the sea.

The storm was just beginning.

The Old one is available from Amazon and all good retailers

About the Author

This is the part where I am supposed to write up some boastful crap in third person about my accomplishments as a writer. I have always found this part about any book odd. Yes, I have written a lot of stories. And yes, I have been praised for some of those works. But none of that really matters. What matters to me is whether or not you liked this book. So, about me: A real person who likes to hear from his readers. What did you think of the book?

Contact me @ www.indie-inside.com
Follow me @ www.twitter.com/indie_inside